LIZZIE'S BLUE RIDGE MEMORIES

For Patty & the Taylor Conservatory Staff,

"To Everything there is a Season."

At one time in Junior High (& later High School) Students & teachers used to joke that a cup of yogurt had more culture than the entire city of Taylor. Times have changed & that is no longer true. Thankyou for leading the way!

Virginia Elisabeth Farmer

"Lisa"

Order this book online at www.trafford.com
or email orders@trafford.com

Most Trafford titles are also available at major online book retailers.

Note for Librarians: A cataloguing record for this book is available from Library
and Archives Canada at www.collectionscanada.ca/amicus/index-e.html

Printed in Victoria, BC, Canada.

ISBN: 978-1-4251-8676-0 (Soft)

*We at Trafford believe that it is the responsibility of us all, as both individuals
and corporations, to make choices that are environmentally and socially sound.
You, in turn, are supporting this responsible conduct each time you purchase a
Trafford book, or make use of our publishing services. To find out how you are
helping, please visit www.trafford.com/responsiblepublishing.html*

*Our mission is to efficiently provide the world's finest, most comprehensive
book publishing service, enabling every author to experience success.
To find out how to publish your book, your way, and have it available
worldwide, visit us online at www.trafford.com*

Trafford rev: 7/7/2009

 www.trafford.com

North America & international
toll-free: 1 888 232 4444 (USA & Canada)
phone: 250 383 6864 ♦ fax: 250 383 6804 ♦ email: info@trafford.com

CHAPTER ONE

A GOOD MORNING

L IZZIE WALKED out of the farmhouse and onto the little grey back porch. The scent of the cows standing by the barn wafted up to the four-year-old's round, little nose. She hopped off the steps and onto the grass, running to the heavy wooden gate. Sassie, the collie dog, wagged her tail and looked up eagerly as if to say, "Adventure? Fun?" The leather latch was beyond her reach, so Lizzie and Sassie squeezed under the fence and ran through the pasture. They ran over the bridge that crossed the stream. Lizzie was not afraid. They ran around the east side of the big pond. Lizzie had no fear. The dog and child climbed over the quartz boulders that jutted out of the hillside. The large rocks sparkled in the morning sunlight. Lizzie was unafraid. Sassie ran ahead as Lizzie walked the last quarter mile, carefully stepping over cow pies. Finally, Lizzie reached the end of the high pasture where the meadow and the woods met. She turned around and gazed at the farm below. It was the most beautiful and breathtaking sight the little girl from Detroit had ever seen. There before her were the pond, reflecting sunlight, the pasture filled with grazing cows, the little white farmhouse, the barns and the winding road.

****

It was just last night that Lizzie's family had arrived at Grandma's house. It was a long drive through southern Michigan and then the flat lands of the Ohio Valley, over the river and into the hills of West Virginia.

Frequent stops were made along the turnpike so Lizzie and her seven-year-old sister Maggie could run around and play and use the restrooms. Mommie and Papa would take the faithful old cat Tony to the edge of the woods, away from the roaring trucks and the parked cars so he could explore and stretch his legs. Then they'd all get back in the station wagon, Tony bounding over to sit on Papa's lap and rest his paws on the steering wheel.

Darkness fell as the little family drove through the hills and over the winding roads. Jenny, the oldest daughter at age fifteen, could no longer read her teen and fashion magazines. She was sprawled out in the back of the car on blankets laid over the suitcases. Papa turned the radio on and they all listened to country music. It was the only thing Papa could find on the three stations that would come in clearly. Then a song came on that Papa and Mommie recognized. The chorus played, "In the Blue Ridge Mountains of Virginia." None of the children had ever heard this tune before but by the second chorus Mommie had the girls singing along.

Finally the family saw a sign on the road. Mommie said, "At last! Welcome to Virginia!" It would still be a long drive through the Appalachian Mountains. Maggie was already asleep beside Jenny. Lizzie's eyelids began to feel heavy and she too, nodded off to sleep.

Then, sometime before midnight, the station wagon pulled into the long, winding drive. The crunch of the rocks woke Lizzie up. The night was darker than Lizzie could ever have imagined. It was so unlike Detroit with its steel grey street lights and factories that always gave a twilight look to her neighborhood. Here at Grandma's she could see every star as Mommie carried her from the car, up the concrete porch and into a warm bed.

The next morning the sun wasn't even up, but everyone else was. Lizzie smelled sausage and biscuits cooking. She listened to Maggie quietly breathing in and out beside her. She listened to the voices of Grandpa Roy, Grandma Zonie, Jenny, Mommie and Papa... and one voice she did not know. She concentrated on what they were saying.

"Well, I tell ya' the milk is fresh! I just milked Cricket this mornin' like I do every day before dawn!" It was Grandma. Lizzie quietly giggled. Grandma sounded like one of the hillbillies on TV. Maggie rolled over but kept on dreaming.

"Mother, whenever I use your cow's milk, it turns my coffee blue!" It was Papa's voice. "Mother," he had said. He called Grandma his mother. Papa had a mommie?

Lizzie tip-toed out of bed. Her bare feet were cold on the hard wood floor. Maggie, awake by now, quietly followed. Lizzie walked to the kitchen and got into Papa's lap. Maggie crawled into Mommie's.

"Papa, do you have a mommie?" asked Lizzie.

"Yes," answered Papa.

"Is Grandma your mommie?" asked Lizzie as Papa nodded. "How can a Hillbilly be your Mommie? You're not a Hillbilly!" Everyone loudly laughed. There were no more hushed voices now that the children were awake.

"No, I am not a Hillbilly, but I was born in Asheville, North Carolina. Grandma still has her accent. I've been up in Detroit so long I guess I lost mine!"

"Her accident?" asked Lizzie, confused.

"No," said Papa, "her *accent*, the way she speaks."

Grandma was putting food on the plates. "Cecil," she said to the man that Lizzie didn't know, "would you like ta' stay to breakfast?"

"Oh, n-n-no," said Cecil blinking. "M-m-my wife c-cooked a good one f-for me. I g-g-g-gottsa d-d-deliver the mail d-d-down to L-l-laurel F-f-fork!" He walked to the door and everyone waved goodbye to Cecil.

After the postman left, Maggie asked, "Grandma, why does he talk funny?"

"Well," Grandma took a long, deep breath before answering, "old Cecil has a stuttering problem. He can't speak too good; but there's not a finer more honest man in the county. He had to get an extra early start delivering the mail today. There was so much rain the other day, he couldn't get safely to Fancy Gap, so he's leaving out right now. He felt so bad he couldn't get it done yesterday."

Suddenly Lizzie asked, "Where's Tony?!" Maggie looked concerned too.

Jenny said, "He's alright. He slept outside your bedroom window all night. Grandma saw him this morning when she went to milk the cows."

"Why can't I just bring him to bed with me?" asked Lizzie.

"Because I'll not allow a cat in the house," Grandma said. "But I will say this, that's the darned smartest cat I've ever seen. Soon as you and Maggie got carried into the bedroom, he trotted off and curled up 'neath the window. I guess he could smell you girls."

Maggie giggled, "Grandma, I don't smell!"

Grandma said, "Everyone has a scent. Dog's are good for smelling the faintest scent."

"Won't Sassie chase Tony?" asked Maggie.

"No, Dear," said Grandma. "Sassie'll chase a squirrel, a rabbit, even a groundhog, but she's got a healthy respect for cats. Besides the two of 'em followed me into the barn and sat side by side like old friends. Sassie can smell your scent on Tony and she knows he's okay."

After breakfast, Maggie went off to watch cartoons with Grandpa. Jenny helped Grandma with the dishes. Lizzie quickly got herself dressed after digging through her suitcase and decided to go exploring. Now here she was, breathing clean air and looking out over the misty hills of Eureka Farm.

CHAPTER TWO

GONE FISHING

LATER THAT afternoon, Papa said he was taking the girls
fishing. He grabbed some cane poles out of the shed: a big
bamboo one for himself and two little ones for Maggie and
Lizzie. Jenny just carried the bucket, her long black hair pulled
tightly into a pony tail. Papa attached red and white little balls
to the fish line.

Maggie asked, "Why are you putting Christmas tree bulbs on
the fishing poles?"

"Those are bobbers," answered Papa. "When a fish takes the
bait the bobbers go under the water, then come back up." Maggie
looked puzzled, so Papa went on. "You see, the bobbers are full
of air. They sit on the water and when the fish gets caught on the
hook, he pulls the bobber down. The air pulls it back up. Then he
pulls it back down with the bait and you know you have a fish!"

Then Papa grabbed a shovel. He handed Maggie and Lizzie
their rods, carried his rod and handed the shovel to Jenny. He
hobbled to the spring house with the help of his crutch. The
girls followed him there, setting their fishing gear down before
following him inside the small concrete structure. It was dark
within the walls and water ran through the little building. There
were some early fruits and vegetables kept inside and a small
watermelon sitting in the water. Papa picked it up, put it under
his arm and carried it out. "That water comes from deep in the
ground out of a mountain spring. It's ice cold year 'round. Before

7

Grandma got a refrigerator she used that spring house to keep her food cold all the time. Grandma bought us this melon at the store. Too early for melons here in Virginia."

Behind the spring house Papa took the shovel and dug for worms. Papa put his shovel to the ground, had Lizzie stand on the edge and dug in, turning over the damp soil, exposing the pink wriggling worms. Jenny scrunched her nose in disgust. Maggie and Lizzie didn't mind. They'd played with worms in Detroit and the slimy, sticky little animals didn't bother them at all. Jenny set the metal pail down so the little girls could put the worms in it. Papa put a little dirt over the tiny creatures to keep them moist. Then Jenny picked up the bucket and the melon. Maggie took her rod and Papa's too. Lizzie carried her own and they all walked the half mile or so to the pond, Papa carefully managing to hobble with his crutch in the high grass. Several weeks earlier, Papa twisted his knee on the job. He had an operation just before he drove his family to Virginia.

They walked through the lower pasture, crossed the rickety bridge over the stream and then gradually climbed a small hill, up to the pond.

Once there, Papa took a worm and placed it on Lizzie's hook. Then he did the same for Maggie and himself. Jenny pulled a teen magazine out of the back pocket of her blue jeans and sat down, leaning on the little overturned silver boat that was left by the pond. Papa soon explained, "Back in the Great Lakes, a man has a reel on his pole. It's like the thing you keep your kite string on, all wound up. It keeps his fishing line from getting tangled and you can cast way out. Here at the pond the water is deep but the pond isn't very wide so we don't need long string."

Papa then took a piece of long grass and pulled it from it's stalk. He placed it in his mouth and chewed on it. Before Lizzie could ask why, Maggie yelled, "Look at that rock! It's big but I didn't see it before!"

Lizzie said, "It's moving!"

Jenny said, "C'mon, that's not a rock, it's a turtle."

"It's a snapping turtle," said Papa. "Be very quiet and still so you can watch it for awhile. Boy, it's a big one!"

The turtle crawled up onto a log, clear across the other side of the pond and sunned itself. They watched it until Lizzie saw her bobber dancing on the water." I got a fish, Papa!" Sure enough she caught the first fish. Papa helped her pull it in. "Why it's a bluegill! Big enough to keep!" Papa patted Lizzie and Maggie laughed. The startled turtle had quietly slipped into the water unnoticed. The rest of the day, they caught fish. Jenny even fished some after reading the same magazine article about the Rolling Stones twice. Lizzie caught the most fish. Papa said she must be charming them on the hook.

After fishing, Papa carved the melon with his pocket knife. They sat on the bank and rested. "This was a good day," said Papa, "but I don't *ever* want you girls playing by the pond alone. You could drown. Promise me you won't ever come here by yourselves."

"I promise," said Maggie.

"Me too," said Lizzie. She wasn't sure what, "promise," meant.

Then Papa stood and stretched. He and the girls hiked down the hill, over the little bridge and through the lower pasture to the house. Grandma was delighted. She and Mama cleaned the fish and Jenny helped to cook them. Grandpa came in from tending to the farm and they all sat down to a fish dinner.

****

After dinner, Maggie sat by the fireplace with Sassie, playing dolls. Lizzie gathered up her plastic toy cows. They weren't much bigger than her fists. They weren't cow colors of brown, black and white, but were red, yellow and blue. Then Lizzie selected some cowboys and Indians and their horses. These plastic toys were brown, white and black. She threw them in a box and carried them out to the spring house. She selected a spot under a big pine tree and plopped herself down. In the setting sunlight, the ground sparkled. There were bits of quartz in the reddish brown soil. Lizzie gathered pine needles for making split rail fences to keep the cattle in. They looked just like the real fences she sat close to. The tiny sticks under the tree made great forts for the cowboys and their horses. Pinecones became trees. The Indians lived by the roots of the big pine.

The cows mooed in the cattle yard as Grandma went out to do the evening milking. Tony was by the driveway, his tail twitching as he watched a bird pecking in the gravel. "Moo, moo," said Lizzie as she played with her plastic cows. The Indians were getting ready to steal them from the cowboys. Lizzie set them all up perfectly. Tony strolled over and meowed at Lizzie. "Be careful!" she said. "I don't want my Indians knocked over by a big mountain lion!" The cat leaped over the toys and landed in her lap, purring. Lizzie hugged the tom cat and petted him.

After a long time, Grandma came back with a couple pails of milk and Mommie called, "Lizzie! Time to come in!" Mommie gave Lizzie and Maggie a bath and pulled pine needles out of the four year old's hair, washing glops of tree sap from her curls.

That night, Lizzie fell fast asleep in the cool sheets. She dreamed of cowboys and Indians. The Indians were stealing Grandma's cattle, who were big, blue and yellow!

The next morning after breakfast, Lizzie jumped off the porch and onto the ground. Tony came around the corner and followed her out to the pine trees. Lizzie skipped around to the other side of the spring house, but suddenly stopped. Her Indian Village was scattered! Her forts were demolished! The cowboys and Indians and cattle were all over the place. The chickens were scratching and pecking at the ground. Lizzie was furious! Tony put his ears back and hissed at the large squabbling birds. Screeching, the child ran at the flock, scattering the whole bunch. Suddenly, just as quickly as Lizzie charged toward the chickens, she turned and ran in the opposite direction. The rooster was chasing her! Tony ran to the porch and Papa stepped off it, gathering Lizzie into his arms. She sobbed and explained to Papa how she spent all last evening setting up her cowboys and Indians and how mean the chickens were to knock them down. Papa explained to her how the spring yard was just full of worms, daddy longlegs and Japanese beatles. He explained they were just getting their breakfast there like they did every morning.

"Next time," said Papa, "Play inside, near your bed, then the chickens won't scatter your toys." Lizzie nodded and gave Papa a hug. As Papa set her down, Tony rubbed against their legs and purred.

CHAPTER 3

RAINY DAY

PLOP, SPLAT, plop. Rain was falling. Lizzie and Maggie sat on folded towels in the entry way by the great, grey porch. The water made a gurgling noise as it traveled along the eves and the spouts. Once in awhile lightning would flash, followed by the sound of booming thunder.

In the kitchen Papa was talking to Grandma about getting a lightning rod for the farmhouse. Papa's voice was bossy. Grandma just replied, "Don't preach to me, Son!"

Lizzie began to sing, "Rain, rain, go away, come again some other day," and Maggie joined her. Afterwards, Maggie taught Lizzie how to do the hand movements to "Itsy Bitsy Spider." Maggie had learned that song in school.

The rhythm of the rain was steady. The sky was grey and there was a soft breeze. The windows were partly open, as was the door, and the girls having run out of songs sat somberly by the screen door. They watched the rain pour from the spouts and gather in little streams that later formed puddles that gradually grew larger and larger. Lizzie pressed her face to the screen and pushed, wishing she could go outside. She caught a glimpse of Sassie and Tony under the rhododendron bush, curled up together. Somehow they were staying dry. Lizzie could hear the patter of rain falling on the thick, green leaves. She could see it trickling away from the cat and dog.

Lizzie sat back and sighed. Maggie laughed and laughed at

her. "You should see your face!" said Maggie. "The screen made a print on your nose!"

Mommie called out, "Don't do that, Lizzie! You might break the screen!" Mommie always seemed to know what Lizzie was doing, even when she couldn't see her. So the girls both sat back a little and waited for Grandpa to return from the barn. He said the animals needed tending to, rain or shine!

It hadn't thundered for a long while, but there was still a drizzle under darkening evening skies. The television wasn't working, because the antenna had been blown askew by the wind earlier that day. Lizzie couldn't play outside, couldn't have Tony come in and was already tired of her plastic cows. The children that Grandma knew from another farm couldn't visit as the creek was running high and travel wasn't safe. Finally, in frustration, Lizzie yelled, "I'm bored!"

In response Mommie had come to the doorway and looked at her girls. "Lizzie, look at you!" she said. "Why can't you stay clean like Maggie?"

Lizzie had been sitting on the floor and pressed up close to the door. She had grease on her hands from the device that kept the door from slamming. Mommie scooped up Lizzie, took her dirty clothes off and plopped her in the kitchen sink and began to bathe her right there! Mommie even used dish soap! Lizzie said, "I'm not a dish!" The bubbles gathered and popped all around her.

Mommie just said, "I didn't want to use a whole tub full of water." Nobody seemed to mind and Lizzie thought it was so fun to look out the window at the rain while being bathed. Again, Lizzie pressed her nose to the screen. Mommie said, "Cut that out! Your nose will get dirty again and you might pop out the screen!"

Soon, Lizzie was clean and smelling fresh. She had a towel wrapped around her. Even though it was not cold, the evening was a little chilly for a fresh bathed little girl, so Papa made a fire in the potbellied stove. Then he and Grandma put on raincoats and went to the cowshed to do the milking.

Mommie put the gas stove on, lighting a cigarette from the

flame and began to warm some milk. Maggie said, "Smoking is a very bad habit, Mommie. I saw it on TV!" Then she began to bite her lip nervously. Mommie took a puff and replied, "Biting your lip is a bad habit too, Maggie. Worse yet, picking your nose is *nasty*. Stop it now, Lizzie!" The child grabbed a tissue from a pretty embroidered box and sat down on Grandpa's leather chair. She was dry by now, but her legs still stuck to it.

Maggie grabbed a chair and dragged it over to the kitchen stove. She was about to get a cookie from the jar when her mother cautioned, "Maggie! If you want a cookie, ask first! That flame could catch your clothes on fire! I don't want you children near that stove without a grownup helping you!" Maggie sat down on the chair and folded her arms.

By the time everyone else got back from the barn the sun was setting over the hills and Mommie had made hot chocolate for herself and the girls and coffee for Papa and the old folks. Jenny had asked for tea, but Mommie couldn't find any, so the teen had to settle for cocoa. "The Rolling Stones like tea," said Jenny. Grandpa grumbled a "Humph!" and shook his head with a smile.

Lizzie felt cozy. She listened to the rain puttering on the tin roof and she realized she really didn't want the rain to go away. Now Lizzie thought how rain really made her feel happy inside. Grandma said this weather would make juicy peaches and the corn would grow tall, but more than that, Lizzie liked the warmth that came from inside her very heart and soul! Maybe it was damp outside, but inside the little girl felt like the wood stove in the sitting room -- glowing and bright. Lizzie knew she would keep that feeling with her for a very long time.

CHAPTER FOUR

COW'S TONGUE

ONE MORNING Lizzie woke up late. The sun was already high in the sky. "Lizzie! 'bout time you got up," said Grandma. "I've already milked the cows and we done had our breakfast." The little girl didn't smile at Grandma. She just sat at the table. "Here's a biscuit an' some milk. Yer' just a city girl, asleepin' in like that. Why, when I was your age, I'da been wupped but good! I never slept in. I'da had the eggs gathered, kindling picked up and put in the wood box an' already helped my mother with the chores!" Grandma didn't seem angry, but Lizzie felt a little scared just the same. She finished her biscuit quickly and ran to join Grandpa at the TV.

Maggie was sitting on the rag rug watching, "The Flintstones." She sat up a little straighter and announced, "I helped milk the cows!" Lizzie felt like everyone was ganging up on her. Grandpa was done with his chores, Grandma was finishing hers and Maggie had helped.

Grandpa laughed. "Heh, Heh, I just love those Flintstones!" he said as he reached into a crystal jar and pulled out three mint sticks. They were white and painted with red stripes, but they were not curved like candy canes. He handed Maggie and Lizzie each a stick. "Thank you," said the sisters as they watched Fred and Barney go bowling on the television.

After The Flintstones, Grandpa got up and went into the kitchen. Lizzie asked Maggie, "Where are Jenny, Mommie and Daddy?"

Maggie answered, "They went down the hill to get some real milk. Papa doesn't like it fresh from the cow. It turns his coffee blue!"

Lizzie got up and followed Grandpa out of the kitchen and down the hall to a cool cement room. In it, Grandma was preparing a large slab of meat to slow cure for the evening meal. She rubbed on the spices and set it into a bowl with vinegar and other juices. As Grandma turned around and watched Grandpa go out the back door, she spied Lizzie quietly standing there, watching. Grandma said, "Well, hello, Droopy Drawers!" She smiled at her granddaughter. Lizzie guessed that Grandma wasn't angry. "This is a cow's tongue. Have you ever seen one afore?"

"No," replied Lizzie. "What are you doing with it? Where's the rest of the cow?"

"Well, I'm getting this ready for supper. The rest of the cow's been put in a freezer. There's hamburger and steaks an..."

"Th- that's where hamburger comes from?" cried Lizzie. "We eat cows?"

Grandma looked at Lizzie, "Why, yes, Child. Steaks come from cattle, sausage and pork chops is from the pigs, chicken is, well, chicken."

Lizzie was horrified. "I didn't know we were eating pets! I don't want to eat Sassie!"

"Now, Honey," said Grandma bending over to comfort Lizzie. "Didn't you know that we get food from the farm?"

"I know now that you get eggs from the chickens and you milk the cows. I know you get beans and corn too, but not *animals!*" cried Lizzie.

"Dear, dear," sighed Grandma. "You caught those fish in the pond and ate them. God put 'em all here for that purpose and we treat 'em good and kind here on the farm. Then they feed us when we have to eat. Some day your grandpa and I will be pushing up daisies and some critter will come along and eat the grass and the daisies. It's all a part of life."

Lizzie didn't know what Grandma meant about pushing up daisies and she didn't want to ask. She looked at the tongue in the crock by the sink. "I'm not eating that!" she yelled and stormed out the door just as Papa and Mommie were walking in.

She ran past Jenny who was reading a letter and carrying a brown paper grocery sack. She continued to run and found

Sassie, burying her tear stained face into the collie's thick fur. She held onto Sassie for a long time. Patiently the dog stayed by Lizzie's side while the little girl took deep sighing breaths. Suddenly Sassie stepped back and looked at the little girl. The collie began to lick away the tears and Lizzie giggled. Sassie's tongue was warm and wet. Sassie was now licking the child's hands. As the "bath" continued an idea formed in Lizzie's mind. She wanted to see a dog's tongue, to feel it, examine it.

Lizzie put her right hand into Sassie's mouth, but the tongue slipped through her tiny fingers. So, she reached in with both hands way down deep and grabbed hold. Lizzie held on tight as Sassie gagged and began to back away. The little girl pulled harder. The collie began to whimper and her fluffy tail was no longer wagging happily. Harder, Lizzie gripped and pulled, the collie digging her paws into the soil, writhing in pain.

Suddenly Papa came out. "What are you doing?" he demanded to know. "Young Lady, you stop that!" Lizzie let go and Sassie scampered under the station wagon.

"I wanted to see what a dog's tongue looked like!" It never occurred to Lizzie that she couldn't simply paste it back in. Papa lifted the little girl over his knee and swatted her a few times. Lizzie screamed and cried. What was the matter? Why was it okay to take out a cow's tongue and not a dog's? At least she would never eat it! She would simply put it back in later. Why was Papa so mad?

"Didn't you know you were hurting the dog?" asked Papa. Lizzie just whimpered and ran off. Sassie ran to her side and they wandered together, finally sitting by the peach trees far from the house. Sassie once again licked the tearful little girl.

"I...I'm sorry Sassie." said Lizzie.

All Grandma could say was, "She's been cruisin' for a bruisin' all mornin'. I don't think she's well."

Lizzie and Sassie spent the rest of the day together in the yard, romping and playing. The collie knew that sometimes puppies (and children) can play rough. She had a big enough heart to forgive.

CHAPTER FIVE

JUNE

IT WAS June. Jenny had quietly turned sixteen on the third with little fanfare and only family gathered. All her friends were in another state. The only gift she got was a little record player with a picture of a boy and a girl embossed in gold, dancing on the inside of the case. She also got three small records to play on it. Secretly, what made her most happy was the birthday card she received from her boyfriend, Waylon. He wrote every week. He had just graduated from high school and was deciding what he wanted to do with his life. Jenny read that card every day.

The month gradually came to the mountains warm and humid. Still the evening breezes were cool. After the farm chores were done, Lizzie's family would sit in the yard with Grandma and Grandpa, drinking iced tea after dinner, which was usually fish caught by the girls.

One evening, after coming home from the doctor, Papa said, "My knee is taking longer to heal than I'da guessed it would. There's no money coming in except for my sick-pay." He hadn't renewed the lease on the rental house and made the temporary move to Virginia so he could heal. What was supposed to be a short vacation was turning into life on the farm. Papa helped farmers here and there when there was light work to be done but it wasn't paying much. His sick-pay checks couldn't last forever.

"Why don't you just move down here, Davey?" asked Grandma. She was becoming very fond of her granddaughters. The thought of them moving back to Detroit nearly broke her heart.

"Well, Mother, eventually I'll be getting back to work. My knee's healing," Papa paused, "slowly, but it will get better. The doctor said it would be a good three months. I admit I don't miss the factory, but I do miss the pay. Maybe I'll be back to work at the end of this Summer." Papa's concerned face was hidden in the shadows. No one knew what to say.

In the distance, the bullfrogs were croaking by the pond. Their deep, moaning song could be heard all the way to the yard and beyond. It was a comforting sound, unlike the traffic noises of I-75 that were becoming a distant memory to Lizzie and Maggie.

Grandpa Roy suddenly broke the silence. "Yeah, it was a night like tonight, with a full moon, when we nearly drowned the teacher." Papa chuckled and nodded. Grandpa continued, "You remember the story, don't you?" Papa laughed some more and said he did. Grandpa told the story to the girls for the very first time.

"I was a scoundrel -- a very bad boy growing up. My father always had a switch ready for me. The teacher was always switching me too. A switch is a long skinny stick, cut off a tree for whipping children. Today's children don't get switched like in the old days but we were switched back then. Well, that old teacher, or School Marm as we called her, switched me for everything. If I looked at her cross-ways she would switch me. I got so mad at her that me and my friends vowed vengeance. The old School Marm lived in a room attached behind the schoolhouse. Every night we knew she would march out to the privy afore going to bed. So, my friends and I moved her outhouse back about three or four feet and waited beneath moonlight. It was in the fall and a lot cooler. We boys waited at the edge of the woods and sure enough, she came out the door, holding her skirts hiked up around her knees and walked to the outhouse. She strolled aways and then...PLOP! She fell into the hole, screaming! We boys ran off and never did get caught for that one! I was surprised to see her all cleaned up, alive and ready to teach the next Monday!

Everyone laughed and Grandpa continued, whispering of one dark night when he and the same boys played a prank on an old man scared of "Haunts and Spooks." The boys had an old deer head, covered with a sheet, balanced on the end of a pole. They made ghostly sounds all evening until the frightened man came out. Then Grandpa's voice became louder. "The old man stepped out onto his porch, a shotgun in his hands. 'Go away, Spooks!' he screamed, firing buckshot over our heads. We ran like the dickens away from that porch!"

The family was laughing and the children begged for more tales.

"Yeah, but the best prank we pulled was at the Spring Dance," sighed Grandpa. "That old schoolhouse was also used for preaching, trials and of course, the occasional dance. I knew one was comin' up so I was ready for it. Just under my seat there was a knot in the wood plank floor. Whenever Teacher wasn't looking, I'd work my heal into that knothole, making it wider. One day I found a big ol' wasp nest in the woods and by that evening found an empty crock big enough to put the nest into. I put a flat board over it. That was the night of the party. I carried the crock in the dark to the schoolhouse and squeezed through the foundation stones, making my way to where my desk usually was and crouched in the crawlspace between the ground and the wood floor. The lantern light shone through my little knothole in the planks. Thump, thump! The people were havin' a good ol' time above me. The fiddlers were a'fiddlin'. The dancers were a'dancin.' I shook up that crock with the nest still in it a coupla' times for good measure and set it on a level stone. I carefully slid the board away, leavin' the wasps to naturally make their way up and through the hole. As I was squeezing through the foundation, I could hear the swattin' and screamin' and people began to run out the door and pop through the windows. I dusted myself off and acted surprised. I never did get caught for that one and never told a soul! I would 've been hung 'fer shore if they'd known I did it... hung 'fer shore!"

After the laughter died down, Grandma said, "Roy, you wicked Devil!" several times and shook her head. For awhile they sat quietly listening to the crickets and the drone of the bullfrogs. When the children began to fall asleep in the yard, they were carried inside to bed.

****

Later on in the month on a Sunday, Grandma, Mommie and the girls went to the church where the Reverend Smith greeted Grandma warmly. Papa had dropped them off on his way to Hillsville. "Zonie, where have you been! We haven't seen you for about seven Sunday's in a row!"

"Tendin' to the farm and these here young 'uns! My son and his family are down from Detroit for an extended visit!" answered Grandma.

Mommie, Grandma, and the girls sat during the service, fanning themselves in the humid pews. Maggie showed Lizzie how to fold the church bulletin back and forth. It was another thing she had learned in kindergarten. When school started in the fall, Maggie would be entering third grade. Lizzie thought her big seven-year-old sister was so grown up and could hardly wait to go to school someday.

Maggie and Jenny were pulled out a couple of weeks early because of Daddy's surgery. He couldn't walk them to school. He didn't feel it was safe for the children to go by themselves since the Detroit Riots. So the family decided to stay in Virginia until Papa healed.

In the muggy church beneath the simple arched windows, Lizzie nodded quietly to sleep. She woke up during the singing, drooling on Grandma's lap.

After the service, the Reverend Smith walked up to Grandma once again. "Zonie, I was just a'wondering, could we use your pond once again for the baptisms this summer?"

"Why sure!" Grandma replied. "You know you're always welcome up to our pond and our home any time a'tall."

While they talked, Jenny was getting to know some of the other teens. Maggie and Lizzie just held their mother's hands and looked tired.

Afterwards they all got a ride back to the farm with Cecil and his wife Millie, who was a plump, happy woman with big curls and a purse that looked like it had been cut from a yellow and green curtain. The grownups sat up front while Lizzie, Maggie and Jenny stayed in the truck bed. The vehicle climbed up a hill and then down, then around a curve. Up, down, swaying, the truck continued, bumping along. Lizzie felt sick and closed her eyes. Finally there was a straight way and Lizzie sat up again, as the vehicle passed fields of hay, corn, cows and beans. Soon the truck pulled into the long driveway. On the mailbox was a cow carved out of wood and a sign that read, "Eureka Farms." Jenny said it out loud.

Grandma looked at it and said, "Home sweet home."

Maggie asked, "What does Eureka mean?"

Jenny said, "It means, 'Look! I've found it!' "

As they stepped out of the parked truck and Jenny helped her little sisters down, Maggie asked Grandma, "Why do you call your farm, Eureka?"

Grandma answered, "This is the farm we always dreamed of having and when we found it here up on the mountain top we shouted, 'Eureka! We found it!'"

Cecil and Millie said their farewells, declining an invitation to come and visit.

"We're expecting our own young 'uns over. You know the Fourth of July is coming and our son has the next coupla' weeks off. He's a'comin' up today with the little family," said Millie. As Cecil and his wife drove off, Lizzie saw Papa and Grandpa carrying shovels. The men had long, sad faces. They looked so weary that Maggie even got tears in her eyes.

Papa spoke first, "I don't know how to tell you this." Grandpa just shook his head quietly, the usual mirth and sly grin absent from his round face. Papa took the girls to the porch. Grandma, Mommie and Jenny followed. "Sassie is gone," Papa finally said.

"Go find her," said Lizzie. Maggie was sniffling.

"I can't just go get her. She's..."

Grandpa finished Papa's words. "I guess Sassie tried to find you girls and crossed the road. She was struck down on the highway and your dad found her when he came back from Hillsville. Sassie's dead and we just got done burying her."

For the next couple of days Lizzie clung tightly to Tony, reminding him to be a good boy and not cross the road. Maggie looked so sad and lost. One morning after another, Grandma would come inside, exasperated. "A weasel got into the hen-house again!" she would say. "Wrung another chicken's neck! I tell ya' I can't have this happen again!"

Despite the dead chickens, Grandma wasn't ready to get another dog just yet. The pain of losing Sassie was too fresh. Still she knew something had to be done or she wouldn't have one chicken left!

One muggy morning, when the air was so still and no breeze stirred the air to give relief, the family was discussing the dead chickens. Cecil was visiting and suggested geese. "Y-yes! G-g-geese I tell you! They'll c-c-call out and tell you there's a w-w-weasel in the h-hen house!"

By that afternoon, Grandpa had brought home four young geese, all white, and put them in the chicken yard over by the henhouse. Within days, the big honking white birds had escaped the chicken yard and were guarding the drive. They were even more frightening than the rooster. If Maggie or Lizzie tried to help Grandma gather the eggs, the geese would flap their out-stretched wings and chase the girls with their necks stretched out, beaks ready to pinch little bottoms.

Maggie and Lizzie would run to the house, gasping and cry-ing. They missed Sassie even more. Even Tony feared the great, white, demon birds. His ears would flatten to his head and he would hiss and growl at them, retreating under the wood stack or some bush.

Then, one day their trial was temporarily over. Papa and Mommie packed their things up. Grandma had her suitcase too. Lizzie and Maggie were told to get Tony. Jenny was carrying her record player. They all hugged and kissed Grandpa.

"We're going to Asheville for the Fourth of July!" said Papa. As the station wagon drove away from the farmhouse, the squawk-ing geese chased it down the long driveway. Maggie secretly hoped a truck would run them over. Lizzie was just glad to get away from them. Tony twitched his tail. The car gained speed.

CHAPTER SIX

FIREFLIES

THE FAMILY traveled in the station wagon along the edge of Grandma's farm. Lizzie saw the cows behind the split rail fence. The wooden posts seemed to go by faster and faster as the car picked up speed. They began to climb the hill past the pond and the woods and then the hayfield. Lizzie began to feel sick. "I don't feel good," she moaned.

Papa said, "You've just got a little car sickness. Don't stare out the window. Look at something far away."

So Lizzie looked at the tree covered top of the hill which suddenly ended. In front of the car stretched a valley. Along the road they could see a little whitewashed convenience store on the side of the road, which they drove past. Down they went and over a stone bridge, passing places called Squirrel Spur and Fancy Gap. Lizzie finally just rested her head on Jenny's lap and closed her eyes.

Mommie said, "Look! There's a sign! We're in North Carolina!"

Still, there was much driving to do and after what seemed all day to two little girls, they finally arrived in Mount Airy. Papa drove the car into a parking lot surrounded by plain looking brick buildings. He picked a shady spot beside a building and left the windows down. Everyone got out of the car. Grandma was a little stiff and sore after the drive, so Papa opened her door and extended his hand to help her out.

Grandma took a deep breath and said, "Thank you." She stood

for a moment and then said, "Now we'll be at Roses Department Store for quite awhile. What do you plan on doing, David?"

Papa answered, "First, I'll give the cat some water. Then I think I'll take the girls to lunch." He poured a thermos full of water into a bowl and placed it in the crate.

"Papa, I want to go shopping with Grandma and Mommie," pleaded Maggie.

"...and I want to look at record albums, not a bunch of old guys on their coffee break!" added Jenny.

Papa said that would be okay and then took Lizzie's tiny hand, leading her to a little restaurant. Papa called it a diner. Lizzie really wanted to go to McDonalds but couldn't see any golden arches any where.

The diner was poorly lit and except for the sunlight streaming in from the large windows by the front entrance, it was hard to see once inside. As Lizzie's eyes adjusted she saw giant fans hanging by rods from the ceiling, circulating the hot, humid air. There were booths along the wall. Instead of going to a booth, Papa and Lizzie took a seat at the counter. The stools were silver and white and to Lizzie they seemed very far off the ground but she didn't worry about falling off; Papa was beside her.

A young, pretty lady walked up to them from behind the counter. "May I help you?" she asked as she blinked her dark, lovely eyes and smiled sweetly.

"Yes," said Papa. "We'd like a hamburger, mine with everything and my little daughter's just with ketchup."

"Those come with fries, Sir. Would you like any thing to drink?"

"Yes, two Colas," said Papa, but Lizzie suddenly said, "Hot chocolate! I'd like hot chocolate!"

"Why, Honey!" said the lady, "It's blazing hot outside and not much cooler in here! Are you sure you want a hot chocolate?"

"Yes, please!" smiled Lizzie.

"Would you like marshmallows with that?" asked the waitress.

"...and whip cream, too!" asked Lizzie.

"Well, a Cola and a hot chocolate then!" said Papa.

Soon they were eating their lunch together. Lizzie thought her hot chocolate was the best she'd ever tasted in all her four years of life. She ate half her hamburger and Papa ate the other half.

After awhile the waitress returned and asked, "Would you like dessert?"

Papa said, "No, thank you." Then he asked, "You seem kind of young to be working here. Just how old are you?"

"Sixteen," said the waitress. "Well, sixteen in two days!" She explained that this was a summer job - her very first.

"Well, I have a daughter your age, but I never thought of her as grownup enough to be working. She's never had a job," said Papa, adding, "Why, she's still a little girl!"

Papa got up and lifted Lizzie, placing her little feet on the floor. "You're a very good waitress," said Papa. He left her a tip and paid the bill at the cash register.

After checking on Tony in his wood crate in the car, Lizzie and Papa walked to a large brick building and entered its glass doors. Together they searched one level and then the next of the Roses Store and finally found Grandma, Jenny, Maggie and Mommie. Lizzie and Maggie were each given a dollar to spend on anything they wanted. Lizzie found some scary looking comic books and Maggie bought some Mexican jumping beans. The beans were actually little bugs that made some tiny nuts move in a plastic case. Both girls had some change left over.

Mommie, Grandma and Jenny were still shopping. Maggie and Lizzie were bored and Papa seemed restless too, so they all took a walk around town. To Lizzie the old brick buildings were nothing special. By then, Maggie was hungry too, but all she wanted was a pretzel with mustard from an even smaller diner. Papa bought a bag of little red pistachio nuts that were hanging by the register and he shared them with Maggie, who had already gobbled up her pretzel. Lizzie didn't want any. She thought they looked too much like Maggie's jumping beans.

Before long, Grandma and Mommie met them in the parking lot. Jenny soon came running with a bag from the record store and they all got in the car and were on their way once again. Lizzie fell asleep, her head resting on Mommie's lap. When she woke up, her curls were plastered to her face with drool and sweat. The car had come to a stop on a hilltop in front of a tiny, white house.

Everyone got out and they were greeted with hugs and kisses by dozens of cousins. "Welcome to Asheville!" said a tall, blonde woman.

"Ann, this is my cousin Barbara," said Papa to Mommie. "This is the girl that could take a spanking and laugh about it, whereas I'd be crying after two or three swats!"

Lizzie had heard about how tough cousin Barbara was, but she didn't seem to be so intimidating. She scooped the little girls up in a great big hug then pointed to a child beside her and said, "This is Jillian, my little girl. She's about your age!"

"I'm seven," said the little girl in the white dress. She had big beautiful eyes and dark curls. Lizzie's curls went everywhere. Pretty Jillian's were so neat and tidy. "How old are you?" Jillian asked Maggie and Lizzie.

"I'm almost eight and my name is Maggie."

"I'm four," said Lizzie holding up four fingers.

Tony came up behind them, rubbing his body all over their legs and purring. He was so glad to be out of the car. "So, Four, what is this?" asked Jillian with a giggle.

"My *name* is Lizzie and this is Tony."

Jillian reached under the porch, behind a bush, pulling out a big orange tom cat. "This is Thomas and he's better than your old, smelly cat!"

"No! Tony is the best cat ever!" yelled back Lizzie.

Jillian set Thomas down and said to Maggie, "Can you play Pie-anna?" Maggie and Lizzie just looked at each other and said, "What?"

"Pie-anna!" squealed Jillian. "C'mon!" She took Maggie's hand, but Lizzie stayed on the porch and stroked Tony. She was still mad at Jillian.

Soon, Lizzie could hear a plinking sound and looked in the open window. She saw Jillian showing Maggie a large upright piano. Lizzie yelled inside, "Tony's the best cat ever!" Jillian and Lizzie stuck their tongues out at each other.

Lizzie sat on the porch, with Tony in her arms, until supper-time. After supper, the men sat around the table talking and Lizzie stayed in Papa's lap. Maggie and Jillian walked up to the old wooden table and asked for a pickle jar. " I don't know, go ask your mother," said Jillian's father. Lizzie slid off Papa's lap and followed.

Barbara, who had been doing dishes with the older women in the kitchen, seemed to be expecting this. She handed each of the girls a jar with holes punched into the top. "Lightning bugs are coming out right about now," she explained to Lizzie's mother.

Jillian's eldest brother Robby had a little two-year-old daughter named Sherry. The little toddler followed the bigger girls outside and tried to catch bugs too. The three girls, outpacing Sherry, snatched bugs from the air, put their fists in the jars and quickly shut the lids again and again. Jillian set her jar on the porch to keep two hands free for catching the lightning bugs. She was good at it.

Maggie said, "We call these fireflies back in Michigan!"

"Well, they're lightning bugs here!" Jillian said, running with two fists full of the crawling, glowing insects. Maggie helped her open the jar and the bugs were shook into it. Maggie, Lizzie and Jillian all left their jars on the edge of the porch and they danced and jumped and twirled beneath the starlight. Suddenly there was a crashing sound and a baby crying. Sherry had picked up a jar and it had slipped from her tiny fingers. She was cut and bleeding on her bare, little feet.

"On, no!" said Jillian, "babies are nothin' but trouble!" By the time the girls got back to the porch, the grownups were tending to Sherry and were cleaning up the mess.

Papa started to walk to the car then. Lizzie followed him. He was getting their suitcases out. In the distance, through the pine trees, there were sounds of drumming and singing. "What's that?" asked Lizzie.

"Oh, It's just the Indians," said Papa, seemingly unconcerned. He shut the car door and began to walk back to the house. His feet made a crunching noise on the drive. Even though it was a warm night, Lizzie shivered. She felt so tiny under the great big, moonless sky.

"Indians! Oh, Papa! Are they going to kill us and scalp us?" Lizzie began to cry.

"Scalp us?" Papa smiled, "No, Honey, they're just having a party like we are! Besides, they are Cherokee. They're civilized. It's not like on television with the cowboys and Indians fighting all the time."

"What's civilized?" asked Lizzie, still doubtful of their safety.

"Civilized, uh... calm, law abiding citizens like us. Besides, I'm part Cherokee, so are you. Jillian's daddy is almost full Cherokee. We aren't on the war path, are we? Why would they be? Don't worry, nothing's gonna' happen to us."

So, if Papa said they were safe, well, Lizzie believed him. That night, with Tony in her arms, she fell quickly to sleep.

****

The next day dawned hot and sunny. It was the Fourth of July. Robby was the assistant groundskeeper of a large estate in town. Since it wasn't open to the public until later that day, he took Papa, Mommie, Jenny, Maggie and Lizzie to look at the greenhouse and gardens on a private tour. The little girls couldn't help but run through rows and rows of flowers and bushes on the grounds but Mommie frequently shushed them and made them slow down. "Be quiet! We don't want Robby to lose his job!" she cautioned. Lizzie smelled the roses and peered at the great mansion. Even though Mommie said she'd like a house like that, Lizzie didn't believe her. How would Mommie ever clean a house that big? She complained about the housework she already had!

Robby escorted them out the back way after they'd seen the estate's beauty. Next, they toured the grounds and outbuildings. They drove through stands of pine trees and around hills, eventually back into town and then out to Barbara's where they all returned to a surprise picnic. There was so much watermelon that Lizzie felt like she was in Heaven! Everyone had their fill and then sat around visiting until the evening. Atop the hill, you could see the town even though it was miles away.

"Boom!" A loud sound from downtown shook the evening air. Jillian's three older brothers hoisted the young ones onto the rooftop of the garage. "Be careful!" yelled Grandma. "I don't want you kids a'fallin' off a'there!" At first, Lizzie was too afraid to go on the roof. Then she saw that even baby Sherry was up there in Robby's arms. Lizzie was lifted up and she sat on an old blanket, watching the fireworks being ignited in town. Sherry began to cry for her mother and was carefully let down to her. Sitting on the rooftop, the bigger girls felt scared and brave all at the same time. The breeze gently rustled the leaves in the trees as Lizzie and her sisters celebrated the Fourth of July with Jillian and her brothers, on a rooftop in North Carolina.

Then, as suddenly as it started, the Grande Finale', the great, last explosion of many fireworks was finished. The girls were handed down into their daddies' strong arms. Lizzie and Maggie got to sleep on the porch in the cool evening breeze with their Papa that night. It was hot inside the house. Tony cautiously left the spot in the shed where he had been hiding all day, curling up between Maggie and Lizzie. There they rested beneath the fraction of a moon that looked like a thin, white smile without a face. They fell asleep to the chirping of crickets and the sound of bobwhite quails calling to their mates.

CHAPTER SEVEN

STICKY SITUATIONS

THE NEXT morning after a delicious breakfast that Barbara prepared, Grandma and Lizzie's family drove back to Virginia. As the station wagon took the last curve of the long driveway, Papa remarked, "What's going on?"

Papa's voice had so much concern that Lizzie and Maggie looked up and Grandma asked, "Why in the world would Roy leave the tractor by the spring house like that?" The old machine was tilted up on its big back tires, the front wheels lifted nearly two feet off the ground, appearing to just hang in the air.

Papa stopped the car. Lizzie and Maggie jumped out of the vehicle, leaving the doors open in their haste. Jenny tried to stop them but they ran past her. Something just wasn't right. Moments later, Grandpa Roy came around the back of the spring house, wiping his brow with an old, red bandana.

That's when Papa saw a rope attached to the tractor. The other end was hooked to an aluminum fence pole which was stuck in a small pit. Grandpa looked a little embarrassed and very exhausted.

"I bet you're a'wondering what happened here." When everyone continued to stare at the tractor in disbelief, Grandpa continued. "Well, I was a'diggin' a little pond for our geese. It was going well enough until I got down about two feet or more and my boots got stuck. I pulled my feet out of the silt and grabbed my boots. I had a dickens of a time getting them out! I wondered just how far this silver mud went down, so I could get past it and dig some more. I stuck the fence pole in and it kept on a'goin'. I tried to pull it out with my hands and had no luck a'tall. So, I got the tractor out, put a rope around the pole's top and put the tractor in gear. I couldn't get the pole out! I put that old tractor in full throttle and that pole wouldn't budge, I tell you! Instead the tractor nearly toppled over onto me. I turned it off, hopped down and got a cold drink out of the spring. I pulled out my tabacca' and chewed it under the big pine tree, trying to calm myself down. That's about when you pulled up."

Papa made everyone stand back as the rope was cut. The tractor landed with a thud and a bounce. Then he pulled at the rope. Nothing budged. Papa tugged on the pole with all his might and nearly slid into the pit. For two little girls to witness their strong father struggling so much, it was an uncomfortable feeling. They always felt their dad was stronger than Superman. Papa said, "What you've got here is quicksand!"

"It's a quagmire," said Grandma. "I've heard tell of cattle getting themselves stuck in the thangs. Best keep them behind the fence." Maggie and Lizzie scooted closer. "No, it's best we keep the girls away from there." She took their hands and walked them to the farmhouse.

The rest of the day, Lizzie and Maggie watched from the porch as the fence was moved away from the spring house with all hands helping, except the girls of course. They were bored and hungry. For dinner that night, they had left over beans and corn bread. Lizzie cried because there were no hamburgers or fries. Maggie would have even settled for more fish, but Grandma was tired. She worked hard with the other grownups to finish the fence so the cattle wouldn't fall into the quicksand and die.

That night, Lizzie fell right to sleep listening to the sounds of the bullfrogs up by the pond and the coondogs howling from a nearby farm.

****

Lizzie and Maggie had seen the corn, now tall and sturdy, grow from tiny, bright green plants to stalks higher than their heads. Grandpa had planted the yellow seeds months ago in the field beside the driveway. Every day the corn was a little taller. Sometimes Tony would walk out of the cornfield with a mouse or a small black bird in his mouth and then he would quickly dash away from the angry geese to hide under the rhododendron.

One day, many cars arrived and parked in the gravel driveway. Other cars parked far away by the road, closer to the pond. People were dressed in their Sunday best and some people dressed all in white. Maggie recognized the pastor and gave a shy, little wave. Grandma explained that today there would be baptisms in the pond. Lizzie wasn't sure what a baptism was. She and Maggie followed Grandma and Grandpa and everyone else to the pond. Papa and Mommie stayed behind at the house and waited. Jenny watched from the fence. They weren't church-going people, Grandma would say.

As the girls ran to the pond, they could see more people climbing over the fence and stepping carefully around cow pies as they walked through the pasture in their high heels and best shoes. Soon everyone arrived. Some ladies had fans that they waved in their faces and on their necks. The men had removed their hats and were also waving these as their brows beaded with sweat. The pastor said a few words and sometimes raised his voice to emphasize a point. His nose turned red and then his forehead. This frightened Lizzie and Maggie. Soon, the sermon was over. The pastor and his youth counselor stepped into the pond followed by about a dozen people, some dressed in white, others not. The men grasped each person, gently pushing them beneath the water and lifting them out again. There was joyous singing as the last person, a young man, made his way up the muddy shore, smiling ear to ear, followed by the pastor and counselor. Soon all the people entered their cars and drove away for a potluck dinner at the church, but the girls stayed home.

Later that evening, Papa was on the phone, looking for work to mend fences or bring in the hay -- anything to provide for the family. Even though his leg was still mending and some money was coming in the form of sick-pay benefits, it wasn't enough to get his family fed and sheltered.

The next day, bright and early, Papa was already gone. Mommie explained that he was helping to bale hay at another farm. He would be driving the hay wagon. The girls wished they could have gone but Grandma said little girls would only be underfoot, so they helped around the house. Maggie swept the porches and Lizzie helped gather eggs. Even with Jenny by her side, Lizzie feared the geese and the angry rooster.

In the late afternoon, Papa arrived wearing a big straw hat. He had used it to keep the sun off his face, but his arms were sunburned where he had rolled up his sleeves. With him was a big plow horse, still wearing a harness.

"C'mon over here girls!" yelled Papa. Jenny declined. She was reading a letter from her boyfriend Waylon. Cards and letters were coming almost every day from him.

"C'mon over," Papa said again, waving to them. Maggie, Lizzie and even Mommie walked over to Papa and the big plow horse. "He's as gentle as a calf," said Papa.

"Are you sure he's safe to be around?" asked Mommie.

"Sure he is," said Papa. "Just don't walk behind him. Horses are known to kick if you walk behind them."

"Where'd you get the hat?" yelled Jenny from the porch.

"Oh, it's the horse's!" answered Papa as he placed the hat on the animal, fitting the holes over its ears. "I needed something to keep the sun off my face!"

"Where'd he come from?" asked Maggie.

Papa said, "He pulled the hay wagon. I left his partner at the farm!" Then Papa lifted Lizzie and Maggie on the old horse's back and told them, "This is Billy."

"Like a Hillbilly!" said Maggie, giggling as Papa led the little girls around. Then it was Mommie's turn to ride. Papa led Billy around the driveway, making figure eight patterns around the bushes. The horse started to push past Papa to the cornfield and Mommie had enough. Papa stopped the great horse and placed Lizzie and Maggie on its back once again. He led the animal away from the cornfield and back to the bushes again, leading it all around while Grandma took pictures. They stopped to pose and Billy set his nose deep into a bush to snack.

Suddenly Papa said, "Girls, I'm going to lift you off."

"Why?" Lizzie whined. She wanted to ride Billy all afternoon.

Then Maggie screamed, "Hornets!" Papa lifted her off, then Lizzie. Old Billy, his eyes wide with pain and fright, stood there patiently. As the last little girl was lifted off, he reared high and shook his head. Papa quickly led him away from the bush as Mommie and Jenny took the little girls into the house.

Later, the girls checked on Billy. Papa and Grandma were tending to his stings and swollen face. "Poor old fella," said Papa. "He waited until everyone was off of him before he reared and bolted. He's a well trained horse."

That evening Papa rode Billy at a slow walk back to the neighbor's farm. Not one car passed them along the road. Shadows deepend as the horse's hooves clopped along, slowly, on the pavement.

It was dark when Papa returned. As he got out of the neighbor's pick-up truck, he could see lights by Grandma's pond and a small fire. The truck drove off as Papa entered the house and asked, "They aren't doing baptisms this late are they?"

"No, they aren't," answered Grandma. "We've been watching for awhile. I'm afraid to wake up Roy and tell him. He'd want to go on up. They look like hippies!" Grandma handed Papa an old, small pair of binoculars. The view wasn't clear, but in the far off firelight, he could see that most of the people had long, stringy hair and wore tie-dyed and Nehru shirts.

"Maybe they're just camping," offered Jenny.

"Camping? They could have asked first," said Papa in a stern voice. "The farmer I worked with today said some of his chickens were missing the last couple days, then yesterday he found a fire, still smoldering, and some bones and feathers. Someone had stolen those birds and cooked them up on his property!" Papa reached for a shotgun and planned to investigate, but Mommie and Grandma begged him to wait until morning and he did.

The next day as the sun came up, the grownups went to the pond and saw a sad sight. There were dead frogs everywhere, missing their legs. Papa swore as Lizzie and Maggie ran up to him.

"I thought I told you girls to stay at the house! Jenny!" he yelled as the teen ran up to the pond, "I thought I told you to keep the girls in the house!" Lizzie and Maggie were horrified by what they saw. Jenny turned away with tears streaming down her face.

"Why?!" was all the girls could repeat over and over between sobs.

"I suppose someone thought they'd have themselves a mess a frog legs at my pond!" said Grandma. Grandpa just shook his head sadly. He wished now that some one would have woke him up. They wouldn't have stopped him from walking up the hill at night with the shotgun.

That evening and for many to follow, things seemed very quiet. There were no bullfrogs to serenade them to sleep.

CHAPTER EIGHT

SURPRISES

ABOUT EVERY other morning Cecil came to breakfast before going to the post office. He always had a story to tell about local news from in town. This was always a welcome visit since the broadcast news from the city and the newspaper didn't have much to say about the little towns and farms. Besides, if you were patient enough to listen, Cecil had some pretty good stories.

He had already spread the news about the bullfrogs to other farmers. None of them had similar trouble; however last spring, an occasional cow or calf was found dead, most likely from the birthing process. Most cows did just fine on their own but sometimes a very young heifer would find it hard to bring her first calf into the world. Other times an old cow would just be too old to bring forth new life.

"Y-y-you kn-know, Z-zonie," Cecil said to Grandma, "Ya-you sh-should get yourself another d-dog! That flock of geese just stays in the d-drive and th-that's fine for an alarm and fer the chicken c-coop, but a d-dog will protect y-your whole f-farm!"

"That's what I've been telling you, Mother," said Papa. "You need to get a dog."

"Th-there's quite a few d-dogs at the pound in M-m-mount Airy," said Cecil.

"Well, I can't say I haven't been considering it," sighed Grandma, "but I'll tell you, I'll have a hard time getting one as good as Sassie." Everyone was quiet then. Lizzie could hear the bull mooing repeatedly out in the pasture. Morning birds were tattering in the yard. Still, there was silence in the kitchen as everyone remembered Sassie in their own way.

Cecil took one long last sip of his coffee and said, "W-well, I'll be off! S-so long, folks!"

Everyone said, "Goodbye."

That day the girls helped with the farm chores and when they were done, Lizzie played in the yard with Tony. He was fat with the wildlife he was catching in the cornfields.

Papa came home early from inspecting fences and grabbed some jars. "Let's catch some Japanese beetles!" He said to Lizzie and Maggie. They picked dozens of the shiny beetles off the peach trees. Papa shook them in the jars and they squirmed and buzzed. Lizzie thought they were so pretty, but Papa said the ugly, greedy little things destroyed crops. They picked a few more beetles and dug up some worms. Then they spent the late afternoon fishing.

During dinner, as they enjoyed the tasty fish, Maggie said, "We saw the turtle again!"

"Why, Honey, you did?" said Grandma. "I wish you'd catch it and we could have some turtle soup!"

Turtle soup didn't sound very good to Lizzie.

"You know," said Grandma, "I have a mind to ask those Thompson children a few farms over to catch that turtle. They're really good about catching thangs like that. Don't know how they catch 'em thangs but they do!"

That evening, Grandma called over to the Thompson's house and talked a long time to Mrs. Thompson. After Grandma hung up she said, "Those Thompson children are going to come over next weekend. They're going to bring games over 'n play after they catch that turtle. We'll have ourselves a little party. Does that sound like fun?" Lizzie and Maggie were happy to hear that! It wasn't easy for children to visit each other in the country unless their farmhouses were close to each other or they went to school. Maggie especially could hardly wait. She missed playing with children.

Jenny asked, "How old are these children?" When Grandma said the oldest was about fourteen, Jenny's mood seemed to brighten. She hadn't seen another teen since she went to church and to Asheville. That seemed like ages ago.

Before bed, Grandma said she had a surprise for the girls. "It's your birthday tomorrow, Maggie. We're going to Mount Airy to take you shopping, but for now I have a present for you." Grandma handed Maggie a gift wrapped up in red paper, left over from Christmas. Then she handed Lizzie a similar package, wrapped in green paper. Jenny got a blue one with snowflakes on it. "Here are sister gifts for you." The girls quickly unwrapped their gifts to find three identical manicure kits, one in a black leather case, one in a tan case and Maggie's in white. Lizzie and Maggie didn't know what to do or say.

Maggie managed to smile and say, "Thank you." The little girls had hoped for toys.

Jenny actually seemed pleased. "Thank you, Grandma!" she said breathlessly. More than the manicure set, she was excited about Mount Airy, but she wouldn't tell Grandma that. She liked the farm, but so desperately needed to get out of the house and see other people, teens and young adults.

Grandma held Maggie's little hands and explained, "Even on a farm a young lady should take care of her nails." Grandma took out a metal file and showed the girls how to smooth a rough nail. She used Maggie's thumb. "You don't want a jagged nail catching on your mending or ripping off on a hay bail. It could get infected and you could lose a finger!"

Then Lizzie noticed. Grandma's hands were always working fast, but now she slowed down enough for Lizzie to really see Grandma's fingers for the first time. The tips of two fingers were missing on one of her hands and the pinky was almost completely gone! "Grandma, what happened to your fingers?!" gasped Lizzie.

"You never knew?" she said to Lizzie. "Well, when I was three years old, not much littler than you, my brother was chopping kindling for the cookstove. He wasn't much older than Maggie -- he was about eight. I thought he was all big and growed up,"

Grandma said with a smile. "I kept a puttin' my hand on the chopping block and my brother told me to keep my hands away. Well I kept a teasin' like that and he yelled for my Ma. She said he was big enough to tell me to mind him and he said he would wup me good if I kept putting my hand on the block. Well, the next time he brought the axe down I didn't draw my hand away fast enough and... whack! There went my fingers. My father was a doctor and tended to my wounds. Then he put my little chopped fingers in a jar and buried them. A part of me will always be in my birthplace in North Carolina. Over time, I got better. I could've gotten infected bad. That's been more 'en sixty five years ago."

Grandma sighed and became quiet for awhile. "Anyway, tomorrow we're a goin' to get a dog! That's the other surprise. We'll go right after we take you shopping for a pretty dress, Maggie!"

CHAPTER NINE

A NEW DOG

ALL NIGHT Maggie and Lizzie tossed and turned. Jenny didn't sleep much better. They were so excited that they were going to Mount Airy with Mommie, Papa and Grandma to get a puppy!

Morning seemed to take so long to arrive, but finally the sun rose. The children couldn't get through breakfast fast enough. They rushed to the car after hastily putting the dishes away.

On the drive, Maggie excitedly sang each and every song she had ever heard and repeated, "This Land is your Land," at least three times. Lizzie quickly became carsick again. Her mother gave her sips of Vernors and the little girl kept her eyes closed most of the time. Finally they reached Mount Airy. The sky overhead was grey and overcast. It was humid. Papa got them all hotdogs for lunch and then they went shopping.

Jenny headed right for the record store, while Grandma and Mommie tried on dresses with Maggie. The birthday girl got a red, plaid jumper and a matching hair band to pull her straight, brown hair away from her face. Oh, but the shopping had just begun! So Papa went to get a haircut and took Lizzie along. Lizzie hated shopping, especially for dresses. She enjoyed being with her father much more.

The barber shop was a brown brick building, like most of the other structures in that town. It had a big, glass window in the front with the words **Airy City Barber Shop** printed in big, gold letters on the pane. A large, red and white pole stood by the door. It looked a lot like Grandpa's mint candy sticks. Inside, the shop had leather seats and a table with magazines. While Lizzie and Papa waited, the little girl looked at the magazine pictures. There were mostly magazines with pictures of deer, fish and guns, another with tractors and plows and one underneath the pile with ladies in swimsuits. "I'll take that one," said a customer and he put it high on a shelf.

Finally, it was Papa's turn to get a haircut. "Do you think you'd like a haircut, too? Mommie's been having a hard time getting a comb through all that." Lizzie's curls were getting long. They were always getting snarled with bits of straw and even sticks getting tangled in them.

"Okay," said Lizzie and she too got to sit up in a big chair, next to Papa and have a cape put around her body. Snip, snip she heard the scissors. Lizzie watched her hair fall to the floor. It curled and settled at the barber's feet.

Soon, the two were all done. As Lizzie left the barber shop, she felt a lot cooler than when she had gone in. She could feel the breeze on her neck as they walked to Roses Department Store to find Mommie, her sisters and Grandma.

Once they all gathered, Mommie looked at Lizzie and just gasped. Grandma said, "What did you do to that poor baby's hair?"

Lizzie's happy smile turned to a frown as Jenny said, "Your hair is short like a boy's!"

Suddenly Papa said, "Hey, girls, let's go out for an ice cream while Mommie and Grandma do some more shopping." So they went back to the diner and were greeted by the sixteen-year-old waitress.

"Well, hi there! I remember y'all. You brought some friends this time?" asked the girl.

"These are my big sisters!" said Lizzie.

"Y'all got your hair cut?" she asked, but Papa quickly said:

"These girls would love to have a banana split."

As the waitress scooped in the ice cream, one scoop of vanilla, one of strawberry and then one of chocolate she asked, "You want nuts with that?"

Lizzie didn't want nuts but Maggie piped up, "Yes!" The waitress poured on chocolate syrup, strawberries, pineapple and then sprinkled nuts all over the top.

"Happy Birthday, Maggie!" said Papa as the three girls dug in with their spoons.

Lizzie really liked that waitress. She made the best hot chocolate and despite the nuts, the best and largest banana splits ever! Very soon the little girls were full. As Jenny finished the last bites, Papa paid the bill at the register. He then gave the girls each a handful of coins. "Give these to the waitress." Jenny gave hers to Maggie and the little girls ran to the other end of the counter.

"Here's your tip!" said Maggie.

The waitress quickly stepped to the fountain area, reaching for something. She turned around and said, "Happy Birthday!" as she handed Maggie a large striped, flat sucker. Maggie's eyes went wide with surprise and she hugged the waitress.

Everyone eventually met back at the car and they drove off to the dog pound. They had to get directions from a policeman because they couldn't find the building at first. After awhile, they located the pound. It was a lighter shade of near yellow brick. An animal control officer led them all behind the building where they saw rows and rows of chainlink fence -- like cages, holding dogs, puppies and a few frightened cats. Maggie saw a fluffy dog. "I like this one," she said.

"No," said Grandma. "That one'll get full of burrs and ticks."

They saw white dogs and black dogs. "Black dogs scare me. They're a bad omen," said Grandma. There were little yapping dogs and big dogs. Eventually they came to a cage with a scruffy, medium sized dog in it. It laid it's head on its forepaws and looked up at them with sad eyes. Maggie paused before the black and tan dog. It shyly wagged its tail, but did not lift its head. Everyone gathered around. Lizzie wanted a puppy. This animal looked all grown up.

"This one is about nine months old, give or take several weeks," said the officer. "We had to take him away from his owner. He wasn't being fed, had no water and we think he was being beaten. He's been neglected."

Beaten -- it was such an awful thing to hear. The officer said this one seemed to be a good dog and not a biter, despite his rough life so far. Papa asked, "This is a German Shepherd, right?"

"Uh, yes... mostly we think," said the officer. "Would you like to take a closer look?" Everyone said yes, and the dog's cage was opened. Papa touched him first and the young dog crouched. He looked up in fear at Papa, but he did not growl nor snap. Mommie patted him and the girls stroked him gently.

Grandma said, "Well, I don't really know..." The dog's ribs showed through his thick coat. Long legs stuck out from his fur, ending in huge paws.

"Well, walk him around a little," Papa said. Grandma took the leash and the dog shyly followed, sniffing around the cages and wagging his tail.

Maggie felt joyful, excited. "I like him!" she beamed. Grandma smiled and agreed to take the dog at Papa's urging.

Grandma signed the papers, paid a fee and got the dog its shots. Out the door they went and put him in the back of the station wagon. Papa had some leftover hotdogs in a bag from lunch and fed them to the German Shepherd. The poor, half-starved dog gobbled the food down fast and wanted more. They soon drove off toward the Virginia border. As they followed the curve of the mountain roads and climbed the hills toward home, the dog suddenly vomited. Up came all the undigested hotdogs. "Eww! Yuck!" Lizzie said. Papa stopped the car and cleaned up.

After they got home, Grandma got out a silver, grey galvanized washtub and put soap and water into it. Papa lifted it onto the picnic table so Grandma wouldn't have to crouch down. The girls stepped up onto the benches. Then Papa lifted the dog into the tub where it patiently had its first bath. Grandma and the girls scrubbed him clean. Grandpa walked by from the barns and said, "So that's what you got. Looks like a fine dog," and he strolled into the house to wash up for supper.

Lizzie saw a piece of corn behind the dog's furry, pointed ear.

"How'd that get there? He's got corn on him," and began to reach up to pick it off.

Grandma stopped her and said, "That's not corn! That's a tick!" As they scrubbed further into the dog's fur, they found he was crawling with ticks and fleas. The little bloodsucking insects were drowning in the tub and Grandma had to make sure the girls didn't get any on themselves. Jenny quit right then and there, putting her rag on the table and shaking her arms and legs.

"I want to call him Kemo," said Maggie. Nobody had thought of a name up until then, so Grandma agreed to call her new dog by that name. Before supper, they walked Kemo around the house and chicken coop, introducing him to the cows, chickens and geese. Lastly, they brought Tony out from the woodpile, onto the front porch.

This was a stranger to Tony. Papa petted the growling cat, holding him tightly, but gently. Kemo's thick, pointy ears perked up and his tail wagged. Papa petted them both and let them sniff each other's scent from his hands. Kemo began to lunge at Tony and the cat hissed, but Papa stopped the dog with the choke chain. Kemo retreated in fear. Papa gently started the process again and soon the two animals began to trust each other.

The girls washed up before supper and Kemo was put up for the night with some food and water. Mommie had cooked spaghetti as a special treat. Maggie and Lizzie fell asleep that evening, their tummies full and their little bodies completely tired.

CHAPTER TEN

VISITORS

THE NEXT afternoon a car arrived. It was Uncle Edward and Auntie Agnes and their nine-year-old son, Greg. The boy wore blue jeans and a red T-shirt and smiled in a goofy way. Along the drive from Michigan they had stopped off at a rest area and Greg caught a tortoise. As everyone hugged and said, "Hello," Grandma looked at the little reptile and said,

"I see you got yourself a tarpin."

"It's a turtle," said Greg.

"No, it's a tortoise," corrected Uncle Edward.

"Down here," said Grandma, "we call 'em tarpins."

"Now we can make turtle soup!" said Lizzie. Greg eyed her and held the tortoise close to his chest.

Grandpa said, "You need to have a big ol' snapping turtle for soup. We can't eat that little tarpin." Greg still held the little creature close to him.

Everyone sat around the yard. Chores were done earlier and evening was fast approaching. Greg allowed the other children to play with "the tarpin." And Kemo sniffed around the tiny animal. It retreated into its shell to hide.

Uncle and Auntie stayed the weekend and then returned to Michigan, intending to leave Greg for the rest of Summer Vacation. The three children found more tarpins along the drive. Lizzie had never paid attention to them before since the little creatures in their shells blended with the rocks.

A couple of days later, Greg, Maggie and Lizzie met five children coming from the pond carrying something in an old grey and red blanket. "Howdy," one of the older children said as they came closer.

"Howdy," another one said.

Grandma came out of the farmhouse, wiping her hands with a dishtowel. Jenny was right behind her. "Well, hello. These are the Thompson young 'uns," she said to her grandchildren. "This oldest boy is Wendell; these girls are Roberta and Darlene. This boy here is Roger and the little 'un here is Richard, but we call him R.D."

R.D. smiled at Lizzie and took her hand. "Glad ta meech' ya!" he said, more to Lizzie than anyone else.

"These here are my grandkids, Jenny, Greg, Maggie and Lizzie," Grandma said. "I see ya' caught that ol' turtle!"

"We shore did!" said Wendell opening up the blanket. Sure enough, there was the turtle, on its back, flapping angrily and snapping its jaws. "Keep away from these here jaws!" said thirteen-year-old Wendell. He seemed to be the natural leader of the children, even though Darlene was almost fifteen. R.D. was the youngest, but he sure wasn't shy. Jenny, Roberta and Darlene went inside to help Grandma prepare the turtle, and Roger carried a medium sized box into the house. R.D. and Wendell stayed outside, petting Kemo.

"You'll have a fine dog there, once he's growed up," said Wendell. "He has big paws." He then stood up and said, "Roger brought all our games with us so we can play."

After awhile, the younger kids followed Wendell into the farmhouse. Soon, all the children were rummaging through the box. Inside of it were games like Candyland, Chutes and Ladders, Hi-ho Cherry-o, Monopoly and at the very bottom, playing cards.

"I snuck those in," said Roger in a low voice. "Mamma says they're of the Devil but my uncle gave 'em to me!"

Once everyone was together, the older kids started right into playing a card game while the turtle simmered nearby in the kitchen. R.D. and Lizzie kept circling around the older children and asking questions. Finally Jenny and Darlene turned around, smiling nicely. "Why don't you and R.D. go for a *long* walk. R.D.'s sweet on you!" said Darlene. Lizzie looked at R.D. who grinned and nodded.

"Go on!" said Jenny. Roberta and Maggie pushed the littlest children out the door. The older boys just laughed.

So, Lizzie and R.D. ran off the porch and walked to the barns, followed by Kemo. The two children walked and talked about tarpins and cows, while they ate green fruit they'd found in the orchard. R.D. taught Lizzie how to jump over cow patties. Lizzie already knew how, but R.D. seemed to make it look like more fun. The children spent a long time climbing on hay bales in the barn, up and over troughs in the milking shed, watching mice skitter along the wood beams. After awhile, they left the barn.

They saw that the sun was about to set. The clouds were feather-like in the orange and red sky. "How old are you?" asked R.D.

"I'm four and a half years old!" said Lizzie.

"When's yer birthday?" asked the boy.

"In March. I remember 'cause I like to march!" said Maggie as she stomped her feet.

"I'm six years old," said R.D. "Ever been kissed?" he asked.

Lizzie replied, "My mommie and my papa kiss me good night."

"No, kissed by a boy, a *lover*?!" asked R.D.

"No, I have not," said Lizzie.

"I think pretty girls should be kissed *a lot*, like on TV," said R.D. "Can I kiss you?"

"Here?" Lizzie asked, a little scared. "Now?"

"No, in the cornfield," said R.D. He took Lizzie's hand and they ran as fast as they could to the cornfield. They walked along the rows of stalks and listened to the cows mooing in the pasture. R.D. kicked the scarecrow and said to it, "You don't work!" It wore an old raggedy shirt and barely moved from the small boy's kick. The children ran through the corn and chased the crows around some.

Lizzie asked, "Do we kiss here?"

R.D. said, "No, not here. Let's keep looking for the right place."

They walked along the rows. Lizzie felt lost. She could hear a brook in the distance. "Here?" she asked.

"Um, almost," said R.D.

They waked around some more. Lizzie guessed that R.D. had changed his mind but he was still holding her hand. The boy suddenly stopped. "Right here!" he said. "Are you ready?" "Okay," said Lizzie. Her heart was pounding from all the running and chasing. She felt a little scared and closed her eyes tightly.

Lizzie felt R.D. softly touch his lips to hers and heard a loud smacking sound at the end of the kiss. "There! We kissed! Let's go tell the big boys!" yelled R.D. He once again pulled Lizzie through the cornfield and back to the yard, where the other children had gathered around Grandma.

"I kissed Lizzie! I kissed Lizzie," chimed R.D.

"Kiss and tell! Kiss and Tell!" sang Wendell and Roger. The girls giggled and followed Grandma out to the barns. All the children were going to help Grandma gather the cows, because the old woman still had the evening milking to do.

"You young 'uns missed supper," said Grandma.

"I missed turtle soup?" cried R.D.

"Well, there's a little left fer ya' but I'm afraid all that's left for Lizzie is a little cornbread," said Grandma with a wise smile. Lizzie was glad. She did not want to try the turtle soup.

As the excited children gathered the cows, the herd began to run. "Now stop that!" yelled Grandpa. "You'll make them dry up and stop producing milk!" The kids calmed down and the cows began to trot towards the barn. Grandpa mostly raised cattle for the meat market, but with all the children visiting for the Summer, he needed the cows to give extra milk.

Lizzie couldn't see how the cows could just dry up. Old Cricket, Grandma's favorite, had milk streaming out of her udder as she trotted along. Soon, the cattle began to walk slowly, heading for the barn and the children quietly unlatched the doors and opened hay bales. Grandma milked her cows by hand in lantern light, complaining about the lateness of the milking and how children ran around all day and didn't come in for dinner.

After the evening chores, Mr. and Mrs. Thompson picked up their children in a large blue pick-up truck. Lizzie's hand-me-down jeans from Greg were all scuffed up and dirty from the barns and fields. There was hay in her hair.

"Who's little boy is this?" laughed Mrs. Thompson.

"I'm a girl!" yelled Lizzie and she stormed off into the house.

"Well, I'll be!" said Mrs. Thompson.

Lizzie watched the pick-up drive away as she looked out the bedroom window. She could barely see the children sitting in the truck bed. R.D waved at her and she blew kisses at him. Then she danced through the house before her mommie could scoop her up and stick her in a warm bath.

Wow, what a day!

****

In late August. Papa's leg was beginning to heal enough for him to return to work at the factory. The doctor said maybe he should go on walks that would get longer every day. "Up and down the road, without the crutch. Maybe around the farm, take a few hills. Just don't jump right into work and standing for a long time. If I were you, I'd give it another two or three weeks," said the physician.

For a week and a half, Papa went on walks, to the neighbors, to the pond, down the road, out to the barns. One sunny morning he took Mommie, Grandma and the children to the woods that bordered the farmland.

"Now, Dave, I don't want you to over do it!" warned Grandma.

"I'll be just fine. I can't be an invalid the rest of my life, Mother. I feel fine. I might even go back to work mid-month, maybe the twentieth at the latest." He moved the top two bars of the spilt rail fence, revealing a path in the woods. Everyone crawled over the wood and into the small forest.

"Honey, the children have to go to school. Couldn't we move sooner?" asked Mommie.

As the family made their way on the trail, Papa answered, "We really don't have a home yet. We'll go up a few days before I get back to work and stay with Edward. I wouldn't even know what school district to put the kids into."

Grandma said, "The young 'uns can go to school here for a few weeks until you're settled in."

"No," said Papa. "I don't want to enroll them just to pull the girls out again. I'll put them in school when I find out where we'll be living."

In the distance, they could hear a stream. It was as if the water was playing a cheerful song. "I guess that's what you'd call a babbling brook," chuckled Papa. "That's the same stream that flows through Grandma's farm."

"Who owns these woods?" asked Jenny.

"Why I do," answered Grandma. "This is a part of my land. We just don't farm this part. It's way too rugged. I let this part belong to nature, to the deer and the rabbits."

Greg was kicking over rotted logs. Lizzie and Maggie were fascinated by the little insects that crawled in the splinters. A little red centipede dashed by Lizzie's feet and she went to grab it. "No!" shouted Jenny holding the child's hand. "Those bite!"

"I've never been bit before!" protested Lizzie.

"You've picked those centipedes up before?" asked Grandma. "Why, one of those big ones wrapped itself around your Auntie Lena's finger a long time ago and stung her, but good!"

"They never hurt me," said Lizzie, but now, because of the warning she was afraid of them.

Papa reached for one little red creature. "I just said how bad those things are and there you go picking one up! Fine example you set for these children!" said Grandma.

"Here," said Papa holding the tiny animal on his palm.

The children backed away at first until Grandma said, "Well, would you look at that!" The children moved closer and saw what Papa had in his hand. It was a little orange newt or salamander. Everyone looked at it. "Well, I've never seen anything like it," said Grandma. It had little gold spots down its sides and sweet, innocent eyes. Papa let Lizzie carry it as they went exploring further in the woods.

Maggie picked up a small branch covered with leaves. "Look at these pretty acorns," she said.

Mommie said, "and look what's under this branch!" It was another little orange newt! Maggie got to hold this one.

A little later, the family walked to the edge of the woods. "Can we keep the newts?" asked Lizzie.

"No," answered Mommie. "We are just visiting their home. We need to let them stay here." The girls set the salamanders down and the little creatures crawled off.

CHAPTER ELEVEN

WHERE'S GRANDMA?

THE SPICY smell of sausage hung in the air long after break-fast that rainy morning. Tony hunched over on the front porch under the awning. Kemo curled up in the shed. The cattle mournfully mooed and stood still in the pasture. Jenny sadly read and re-read the letter that Cecil had brought to her the day before. Waylon had written that he joined the Marines and would be leaving for training soon.

Grandpa stumbled in from doing the morning chores, and when he removed his raincoat, he held a hand near his belt. "That burning pain is back, Zonie," winced Grandpa.

"Roy," said Grandma, "It's about time you went to the doctor." Grandma rinsed off a dish and put it in the rack.

On rainy days, things slowed down. Fences couldn't be mended and hay couldn't be cut. Only necessary things like feeding the livestock or gathering the eggs were done.

It was also a Saturday, so Grandpa put on the TV and adjusted the antenna. He took four peppermint sticks out of the crystal container, handing one each to Maggie, Lizzie and Greg. He stuck the last one in his mouth and they watched Bugs Bunny and Road Runner. Grandpa laughed a little. Later, The Flintstones came on. By that time, the children had finished their candy and were eyeing the crystal dish for more. Grandpa was chewing his tobacco, a nasty habit. Lizzie wrinkled her nose in disgust as Grandpa bent over the side of his leather chair and let go some tobacco juice into the spittoon. He looked like a big grasshopper with a mouth full of brown juice. As they sat and watched the cartoon, Grandma went out to gather the eggs by herself, nearly stumbling over a tearful Jenny who was by now huddled on the porch, her legs damp from the drizzle.

Grandpa watched The Flintstones with the children, but whenever he laughed, he would grab his side and give a painful look. When the cartoon ended, Grandpa turned off the television and looked through a farmer's catalogue. It had plows and other contraptions in it. The newest and best farm implements were advertized, but Grandpa just looked at the pages wishfully.

Maggie and Lizzie played cows, cowboys and Indians with the plastic toys. Sometimes Greg would knock them over with a ball. He acted like he was bowling. After awhile he grew bored of teasing the girls and walked to his room.

Mommie walked in later and asked, "Where's Grandma? It's almost lunchtime and I can't find her!"

Grandpa said, "You know, she *is* taking a long time to gather those eggs."

Mommie found Jenny on the porch. "Have you seen Grandma?" In the distance, by the chicken coop they could hear Kemo barking. Mommie grabbed a raincoat hanging by the door. Papa who had been in town buying the paper and some cream, drove up right then. He set his purchases down on the kitchen table and quickly went out to the chicken coop with his wife.

Not long after, they came back, half carrying Grandma. The side of her coat and dress were muddy and she could only manage to put weight on her left leg. "What happened?" asked Grandpa. A look of worry crossed his face.

"Well, Roy," she began, "I went out to gather those eggs. You know how I always teach a dog to sit and wait until I go through the gate, then the dog is supposed to go? Well, I've been teaching Kemo. He did real good going in. He didn't chase the chickens at all...but coming out I had all those eggs. As I was about to go through the gate, Kemo spied himself a groundhog and off he went, hitting my side a little. I slipped in the mud and lost my balance and felt a pain in my leg as I hit the ground. I twisted my ankle, that's all.

Everyone looked at Grandma's right leg. It was swelling and off to one side a little. Papa and Mommie helped to clean up the old woman before taking her to the doctor. They knew a long, slippery drive from off the mountainside awaited them. Before they left, calls were made and that evening the Thompson girls were over doing the milking.

The girls were over again in the morning, but couldn't stay to visit. They had chores of their own to do at home after church. Jenny helped out as much as she could, but mostly told the children to stay out of the kitchen while she cooked. Grandma had been sent to the hospital and was there the next day, so Lizzie's parents were staying in town. Grandpa was doing extra farm chores. Greg, Maggie and Lizzie were bored. They were left to themselves.

Greg would be leaving for Michigan in a few days. School started after Labor Day and he wanted to spend every moment having fun, so he suggested they catch a fish dinner at the pond. They took some biscuits left over from yesterday's breakfast with them and picked some peaches. Off they hiked to the pond.

There they sat for a couple of hours, listless and bored. With the exception of one boney little fish that Lizzie had at the end of her hook, the fish weren't biting at all. Greg looked at the pathetic little critter and said, "It's too small," throwing it back into the water. Lizzie gave Greg a mean look, but the little bluegill was gone.

The children decided to hike to the cow barn and play. "Maybe later this evening the fish'll be hungry for worms," said Greg. So they all set off for the barn and had a picnic lunch of biscuits and fruit. When they were finished, they climbed the hay bales to the top of the barn and looked out a tiny window near the roof. The air at the top of the barn was hot and suffocating. They opened the window. They breathed in the mountain air, mingled with the scent of cow manure and sweet hay. They rested atop the hay bales and talked.

"Your Daddy says his leg's getting better," said Greg. "You might be headed back to Detroit before school starts."

"I don't have school," said Lizzie. "I'm still too little."

Maggie said, "I don't even know what school I'll be going to. I went to Holy Cross for kindergarten through second grade, but we'll have a different house and maybe a different city when we move back."

"Yeah, I know," said Greg. "Your boxes are in my dad's basement. He says you're all fools if you move back to the city – and you should buy a gun!" The girls shuddered at this thought. As much as thinking about a masked robber scared them, Papa shooting a gun scared them more. So they sat there in silence.

After sitting there drowsily on the hay for a long time, Greg suggested they gather up the loose hay and make a pile. "Then we can jump in it!" he said. They spent the rest of the afternoon falling into the loose hay, flattening it and bunching it up again. Lizzie was too afraid to jump from any higher than two bales. Maggie and Greg jumped from several bales higher. Lizzie grew tired of the game, leaving the other two children, jumping and squealing behind her. She reached into her lunch bag to find a biscuit and noticed the cows gathering by the barndoor. Grandpa was late and the cattle were hungry.

Lizzie reached out her hand. It held half a biscuit and a spotted cow took it gently. She reached out to pet the cow, but the animal rolled its eyes and shied away. She then held out a piece of peach and Old Cricket took it. She patted Cricket who just stood and chewed.

Soon the children saw all the Thompson kids walking up from the distant farmhouse. They showed Greg, Maggie and Lizzie how to feed the cows. Roberta and Darlene did the milking and afterwards they all went fishing together.

R.D. and Lizzie walked around the pond. "You ever catch tadpoles?" asked R.D.

"No," answered Lizzie.

"It's easy," said the boy. "You scoop 'em up in a bucket, pour off the water and put 'em in a jar. If ya' don't have a bucket, you can use your hands, but they slip through your fingers too easy." Together, they caught some tiny tadpoles. After the bigger kids had a couple of buckets full of fish, R.D. and Lizzie let their tadpoles go.

They all hiked the long trail from the pond, over the foot

bridge and the stream, through the lower pasture and onwards to the farmhouse.

Kemo scampered under the wooden gate to meet them and wagged his tail. Greg opened the gate and all the children walked through. He carefully latched it back and they all went into the house.

Grandma was home and Lizzie noticed something odd: Grandma's bed was set up in a corner of the sitting room by the wood stove; close enough to keep Grandma warm, but far enough as to not catch the bedding on fire. Lizzie and Maggie ran to Grandma as she lay in bed and they hugged her gently. Papa explained that Grandma had broken her leg. It wasn't a simple sprained ankle. All nine children signed Grandma's cast while Mommie cooked the fish. It was dark by the time they ate supper.

CHAPTER TWELVE

BACKFIRE

GREG WENT home a couple of days later. Maggie almost envied him. He would be going back to school and making new friends. Maggie complained during the day and at night fussed and fidgeted in bed, keeping Lizzie awake.

All that night Lizzie was alert, hearing the distant howling of the coonhounds from a nearby farm in the valley. The occasional moo of a cow reached her ears. Close to dawn, the rooster yodeled his morning greeting over and over again. Sometimes the geese would honk and then there would be silence. The quiet in between animal sounds made Lizzie feel small and helpless. She could hear Grandma's labored breathing coming from the sitting room. Only a thin wall separated them.

Papa left early that morning for a job. Mommie was up, cooking. She was making French toast and it was a welcome change from the biscuits and gravy with sausage they had most mornings.

Lizzie and Maggie looked out the window. All around was a mist rising from the streams and warm pond into the cold mountain air. The fog gathered around the trees and pooled in the valleys. To Lizzie, it was swirling, mysterious and beautiful. As the sun rose, it barely showed through the ever thickening vapors.

Grandma hobbled out of her bed with the help of a crutch and everyone gathered at the kitchen table. There wasn't much conversation while the family quietly ate.

Finally, Grandma broke the uncomfortable silence. "Well, I must say, it's nice to be waited on fer a change. I need to get the recipe for that French fried toast. That was *so* good! When I'm a feelin' better I want to make it." Soon everyone began to talk. It seemed Grandma would be all better. Lizzie and Maggie were glad.

As the family cleared the table, there was a clopping sound coming from the road. Grandpa and Mommie helped Grandma up and they looked out the large parlor window. Everyone was watching as large brown forms appeared out of the fog and the sounds became louder. There were three girls on horseback coming up the road. Soon the sound of crunching gravel could be heard and the family walked out to the large front porch. One girl, who wore her hair in a long black braid dismounted. She carried a package to Grandma.

"Mrs. Farmer," said the girl, "Mamma wanted me to bring you by this ham. Maybe your family can cook it later. Mamma and Paw wish you well and hope you get better real soon." Grandpa took the ham as Grandma thanked her. Then the girl rode away with her companions back into the swirling mist.

As the family entered the house, Grandma explained that the girl, Laurine, was only sixteen and would be getting married next June. Jenny thoughtfully listened as Grandma said, "Then again, I was a month shy of eighteen when I got married."

Later that morning the mist had burned off and the day promised to be hot and humid. Outside the sitting room window, the blackbirds gathered. They were chattering away incessantly. The birds were so bold that they would swoop down and threaten Tony. Grandma sat in a rocker. She watched the birds and listened to the racket. "David," she said, "I want you to chase them birds away! They're just about driving me crazy! They aren't singing a 'purty' song; they just chatter away and I'm about to lose my mind over it!"

Papa had come home early for lunch as there wasn't much work to do on the neighbor's farm. "Well, Mother, I was going into town to buy a gun anyway. I'll get a B.B. rifle and shoot at them. They're bound to move on."

After a quick meal of soup and ham sandwiches, Papa gathered up Mommie and the kids but at the last moment Lizzie decided to stay. "I want to stay with Grandpa," she said.

"It might not be such a bad idea if you stay," said Papa. "Well, you help Grandma if she asks you." Papa got in the car and slowly drove out the gravel drive.

Together, Grandpa and Lizzie cleaned up the kitchen and tended to little jobs for Grandma. The old man took the child out to the barn, showing her the big black rat snake that lived in there. "You won't never see it if you don't know where to look!" he said. He also showed her a little fence lizard and explained what a salt lick was. Over in the lowest part of the pasture, there were white bricks about the size of cinder blocks in wood boxes. The cattle liked salt and Grandpa explained they couldn't use a shaker to put salt on their hay, so they'd come and lick the salt blocks. Grandpa also had a big hemp rope tied between trees. Lizzie saw a cow rubbing it's itchy back on the fraying rope. "Since they can't reach their backs with those hooves, they scratch their fly bites on that," said Grandpa.

As they turned from the pasture, they saw a pick-up truck drive on the gravel to the house. It had a hardtop camper over it. The truck stopped and out hopped a handsome young man followed by a yellow Labrador. "Well, Jerry!" yelled Grandpa. "You made it!"

"I sure did!" said the young man. "I came to help out." He looked at Lizzie and asked, "Who is this?"

"This is Dave's girl, Lizzie," said Grandpa.

Jerry set her on the fence and looked her over. "Humm, skinny looking thing." He left her there as he and Grandpa walked off to look over the farm. Lizzie scampered down as Kemo and the yellow dog sniffed each other. The dogs followed the two men and Lizzie quietly stayed in the shade. Kemo and the other dog began to fight. Jerry yelled, swatting them both, picking up his dog. He threw the snarling Labrador into his truck, shutting the hardtop, leaving the windows open slightly.

Off the men went, followed by Kemo as the dog in the pick-up yelped for Jerry. Lizzie followed closely behind, staying quietly out of the way. They walked all over the farm as Grandpa explained about feeding the cows and doing other chores. Then they talked about pheasant hunting and other subjects that Lizzie found boring, but she enjoyed spending time with them.

When they returned to the yard, storm clouds were gathering over the hilltops. They still hadn't reached the house. Papa had taken Jerry's dog out of the truck and was giving it water. "What are you doing with my dog?" asked Jerry.

"Don't you know any better that to leave a dog in the back of a hot car in the direct sun on a hot day like this?" yelled Papa.

"That's my dog and I know what I'm doing!" scowled Jerry.

Away from the men, Mommie explained that as young boys, Papa and Cousin Jerry never got along and argued every time they saw each other. Jerry yanked his dog back and Lizzie's father stormed into the house.

After awhile Papa walked back outside and shot the B.B. gun into the trees. The blackbirds scattered but soon gathered again. He shot into the trees, not aiming at any birds, intending to frighten them off. Jerry walked up behind Papa, startling him as he said, "Now, what did those little birdies do to you?"

Papa growled, "They're bothering my mother!" He then brought the gun down and icily said, "You're one to talk. You shoot ducks and pheasants."

"Yeah, " retorted Jerry, "but I eat them!"

Lizzie was perplexed. This wasn't going well at all. She liked Jerry. She loved her papa. There they were, arguing and Lizzie couldn't understand why. Papa aimed the gun and once again fired at the birds. They flew off momentarily.

Papa stomped back into the house. He came out again with a box of targets. Mommie, who had been waiting outside, carried a handgun and began to walk. Lizzie and Maggie followed their parents to the upper pasture past the cattle and almost into the woods.

Their dad had bought the guns at a pawn shop in town. He wanted Mommie to be safe when they moved back to Detroit because there were so many houses being broken into. It had already happened to them once, years before, when Papa was at the factory: Mommie was in the kitchen. She had fooled the robber by saying her husband was home from work, sleeping in the next room. Then she yelled, "David!" and the stranger left in a hurry.

Lizzie realized with the purchase of the gun that her parents fully intended to return home to Michigan. She wished she could just stay on the farm.

Papa nailed a target to a large, half dead tree and told the children to stay behind the adults and be quiet. Mommie listened to Papa as he explained to her how to fire the pistol. She fired and hit the target, but not even close to the center. She aimed and fired once again. Papa said, "You're getting closer to the bull's-eye," and sure enough she had hit closer to the middle. The children watched closely now. Lizzie hoped this time her mother would hit the very center. Mommie aimed the gun and pulled the trigger. There was a small puff of smoke and a sound like a small firecracker. Mommie screamed and fell back. Something black was between her eyebrows and blood was making a small stream down her nose and onto her cheek.

Papa helped Mommie stumble back to the farmhouse as Lizzie and Maggie tearfully followed. They walked through the door and Jenny's eyes became wide with terror. Their mother was quickly moved past Grandma who was resting in the sitting room. Papa gently carried Mommie to the bedroom and put her on the bed. He then put the gun on top of a high dresser.

Jerry took a look at Mommie and said, "Looks like the gun just backfired. It's not a bullet but a fragment."

"Don't you think I know that?" yelled Papa. By now, heavy rain had begun to fall. It was too long and dangerous a drive off the mountain to go to the doctor. The steep roads could become slick in rain like this. Papa wasn't even sure the clinic was still open. It was already long past six o'clock.

Grandma told Jenny where to get some tweezers, cotton and alcohol. The sobbing teen found the items and took them into the bedroom. Then she retreated into the sitting room with Grandpa and Maggie. Jerry and Grandma watched through the doorway and Lizzie cowered at the end of the bed and watched Papa carefully run the alcohol dampened cotton ball over Mommie's fore-head. He made sure none of the liquid went into her eyes. He cleaned the shallow wound then delicately picked the metal out from between Mommie's eyebrows.

"It's like a big splinter," Papa said. He worked at it and fi-nally removed the fragment. He showed it to Mommie and then wiped the wound clean. He put a bandage on it and gave her an aspirin.

Jenny was close to hysterics by then. First, she heard that Waylon was joining the Marines. Then Grandma broke her leg. Then the huge argument between Jerry and Papa. Now this! Mommie could have lost her eyes! "I don't know how much more I can take!" screamed Jenny.

"You just have a little cabin fever, Child," said Grandma. "When you get back to school and see young people your age, you'll feel better."

"That's just it," said Jenny, tears welling up in her eyes. "I don't know where I'll be going to school or when. I can't even go to school back home if there's a teachers' strike. I got a letter from a friend. Her mother is in the teacher's union and she says they might strike!"

Mommie came out of the bedroom. "What's all this about? Don't worry until you have to."

Jenny went on, "Mommie, you're so lucky you have us! With Waylon going in the Marines, his mother Verlene doesn't have anyone to watch out for her. She's all alone! What if she broke her leg like Grandma? What if a bullet went into her like it did to you, Mommie?" The teen's eyes were pleading. "Can't I just move to California and take care of Verlene and go to school there?"

"Absolutely not!" said Papa angrily. "Besides, Mommie wasn't hit by a bullet, just a small piece of metal. Stop screaming and just watch these children! You're making them cry."

Everything was slowly darkening. The storm had gathered over head. Thunder and lightning rumbled and flashed over the mountain top. It seemed to be matching Jenny's sour mood. The wind gusted and roared outside. Lizzie was crying, but not about Jenny. It was because Tony was out in that mess. She begged to have her cat come in but everyone was too worried and short-tempered to really listen to the little girl. The electricity flickered out completely as Lizzie sat in the rocker and sobbed. Everyone gathered in the sitting room around Grandma's bed. The only light they had came from the lightning bolts outside. Papa started a fire in the wood stove, despite the stagnant heat accumulating in the house. They sat quietly and listened to the storm.

Crackle! Flash! With no warning, the house lit up like daylight. There was an arching blue light dancing along the barbed wire fences, in the trees and all around them. Little balls of electric light shot from the outlets. The family moved to the center of the room, huddling away from the walls. Grandma sat in a chair with her leg propped up on an ottoman. The girls gathered under a blanket. Mommie sat with Papa and Jerry sat in an old ladder back chair. Grandpa chewed his tobacco, hunched over in his leather chair. He calmly stared into the firelight as they waited for the storm to blow over.

An hour later, when the power came on and the weather was less frightening the family moved to different rooms. Grandma went out to boil some water in two kettles. Jenny and Maggie followed. Papa stood up to leave, glaring at Jerry, and went into the kitchen to sit down. Grandma returned to her bed and got comfortable. "Davey," she yelled towards the kitchen, "let me know if you hear the whistle before I do. I'm heating water for hot chocolate and coffee."

Suddenly, there was a high pitched scream from the kitchen. Mommie and Lizzie rushed in to find Papa hitting and beating Jenny.

"Stop that!" Mommie yelled. Her strength came back to her in a moment of motherly, protective rage. She rushed for Papa thinking he had lost his mind. Then she saw it. A flame on Jenny's back. Papa was using a kitchen towel to beat it and try to extinguish its deadly potential. He managed to kill the flame. Mommie removed Jenny's melted nightgown. A small piece of flesh on the teen's shoulder about the size of two fingers was blackened and blistered. Otherwise, Jenny was fine.

"What happened?" said Grandpa. He stood in the kitchen doorway, holding his side and gasping for air.

Jenny sobbed, "You all told the kids to never reach for a cookie, so I went to get them some. My nightgown caught on fire just as Papa sat down."

Papa said, "I didn't even realize she was up there reaching over the stove." Then to Jenny he said, "We meant you, too! We don't want *any* of you kids reaching over the flame on that gas stove!"

"But I'm not a child!" insisted Jenny. "I'm sixteen! Don't you see that other sixteen year olds are engaged, working, going to school?!"

"We'll talk about this later," Mommie said.

"No, I want to talk about it now," cried Jenny. Her mother just gave her a look that made her stop arguing.

Mommie put the littler children to bed. It was late. The thunder wasn't more than a distant rumble. Lizzie snuck out of bed and opened the window. Tony wasn't under it. The grass was wet. She whispered, "Here Kitty, Kitty." Nothing happened. "Here, Kitty, Kitty," she repeated. Tony hopped across the lawn. He was dry, except for his paws. Lizzie thought the cat must have spent the evening in the tractor shed. The little girl reached down to pet the tom cat. As she stroked him, she reached down and snuck him in.

Lizzie returned to bed. She could hear Mommie and Jenny talking. "We'll talk to Daddy tomorrow. It's a long drive to the doctor. Let's hope we have good weather for it."

CHAPTER 13

BUZZING RUMORS, FACING CHANGES

THE NEXT morning dawned bright and sunny. Papa drove Jenny and Mommie to the clinic in Hillsville. When they came home to the farmhouse, there was good news and bad news. Mommie was just fine. She would most likely have no scar at all. The doctor said he probably wouldn't have treated the wound much differently. Jenny on the other hand had a third degree burn. It was small but could easily get infected. Jenny was given a shot and medicines to put on the wound. "It really hurts today," said Jenny wearily. "I have to take these horse pills too."

Jenny looked at Mommie as if she were expecting her mother to say something more. She looked at Papa and he quietly walked out of the room. Mommie put Maggie and Lizzie in Grandpa's old leather chair. They were all alone with Jenny. Grandma was sitting out on the front porch getting fresh air. Jerry was out doing chores with Grandpa.

Mommie said, "Jenny is moving to California. Even though we are moving back, soon, it won't be soon enough. Jenny is in high school and can't miss so much. She'll fall behind her peers." It was as if Mommie were making excuses or trying really hard to convince herself. She looked longingly out the window.

"When?" asked Lizzie. "When do we go back home?"

"Soon as the doctor gives your father the OK to go back to work. That could be in another two weeks, or so," said Mommie. She turned back to face her daughters. "Anyhow, Jenny is in high school and can't wait forever for school to start. She can't wait around for Papa to go back to work or for us to find a house and a school district to move into. She needs to get that wound treated properly. The University of Michigan would be the best choice, but we are not in Michigan... so," Mommie paused," Jenny is going to move in with Waylon's mother. Verlene is very frail and Jenny can help around her house. At the same time, Jenny can go to school and get her burn treated at a real hospital. Auntie Margaret lives out there and can keep an eye on things. We already called Verlene from the doctor's office and it's all worked out. We just need to get Jenny her tickets for the flight."

Lizzie and Maggie really didn't know what to say. Maggie started crying, "Don't leave!" Lizzie just sat and watched her sisters hug and cry. She leaned over and hugged Jenny around the waist.

Two days later, Jenny had packed her suitcases and moved to the land of her dreams: California; a place with beaches and Hollywood stars that most teens could only dream about. Lizzie's big sister called one evening. She had enrolled in the local high school, the same one Waylon had attended. She had to get a lot of permission slips and have legal documents signed to go to the school without her parents living in Stockton. She was a little frustrated but happy at the same time. "I know when I was visiting Auntie, all I could think about was Waylon, but it never occurred to me just how far I am from any beach, let alone a decent one! It takes at least two hours to get to Santa Cruz and I don't know anybody I can go with." Still, she was excited. When Grandpa got on the phone and asked if she had met the Rolling Rocks, Jenny just said, "No, Grandpa. They are the Rolling Stones and I haven't met any rock stars yet!"

****

Later that week, the family went back to the doctor. Grandma got her cast off, and Papa was given the good news that his leg was completely healed. After taking Grandma's bed apart, he removed the mattress and parts out of the sitting room. Mommie folded clothes as the family prepared to return to Michigan.

They packed their belongings for the long drive home. They just needed to go into town to get gasoline. Papa didn't think any gas stations would be open before dawn when they would be leaving for home. So the day before the big trip home, he drove Grandma, Mommie and the girls to get gas and some ice cream cones.

That afternoon as they returned to the farmhouse, before Maggie and Lizzie could get out of the car, they witnessed a funny thing: Grandpa was running around the house followed by a swarm of bees. Maggie laughed, "I didn't know Grandpa could run so fast!"

Papa answered calmly. "It's like this every time with the bees. He pokes them, prods them, hits their hives with a stick. I tell him, 'treat 'em gently and they won't sting' but the stubborn ol' cuss just won't listen!"

Grandpa came around the corner and dove into the house. Papa, Mommie and Grandma went in another way, Lizzie and Maggie sneaking in behind them.

Grandpa told Papa a new swarm of bees followed a queen into a tree and he wanted to move them to an empty hive. When he approached the hives to get an empty one, his bees became excited. He never could get the empty hive to the new bees.

Papa waited. Close to evening he gathered some dusty things from the closet in the shed. He donned what looked like a safari hat with a veil netting and put long, thick gloves on his hands. Then he took large rubber bands, fastening them over the gloves. He put two more bands over the cuffs of his pant legs and put his boots on. This way no bees would sting him or enter his clothes. He reached for some things on a shelf. He took what looked like a small kettle and put into it some dried weeds that had been hanging near the shelf. He stepped outside and set these weeds on fire, quickly shutting the lid of the kettle. This kettle-like thing he called a "smoker." Papa explained to Maggie and Lizzie that a neighbor, Mr. Shoemaker, had taught him how to gently tend bees. "They'll be gentle as kittens if you don't stir them up and scare them off!"

Papa, all dressed up in his beekeeping costume, took a broken paddle leaning on the side of the shed and walked to the tree behind the house where the swarm waited. He reached out to the bees. Lizzie and Maggie waited a distance, watching with curiosity, mixed with anxiety. They didn't want to get stung! In the twilight, it was hard to see everything. Lizzie spied the wriggling mass of insects. They had clumped together, at the end of a branch, in a ball-like shape to protect their queen. Papa had a large can and gently worked them in. "C'mon, Ladies, get in the can." He reached the larger queen, scooping the workers around her. The remaining worker bees followed her in and Papa carried them patiently to the hive on the other side of the farmhouse. Then he guided them with the paddle into their new home. Once the queen was inside, the other bees followed her into the hive. He secured the lid, slowly walking away.

Papa changed out of his beekeeping clothes. He put them away in the shed and quickly washed up in the house. Maggie and Lizzie had been waiting nearby, holding onto Kemo's collar so the dog wouldn't snap at the insects. Papa came outside again, carrying a note. Grandma and Mommie brought out some lemonade. "I think you can let Kemo go now," Papa said. The Shepherd scooted under the picnic table.

"Roy's a little sore after his ordeal," said Grandma.

"Did he get stung?" asked Lizzie.

"No, Honey," said Grandma. "His side's a'hurtin'. We'll take him to the doctor on Monday. You won't be here, David, so I'll have Cecil take him in."

"Mother, I can take him," said Papa. "My foreman called. Dad left a note by the phone saying to give the boss a call. There's a strike."

"Well, then, I'll have you take him into town to see the Doc," said Grandma. "He's jes' got a stitch in his side. Maybe he can get some medicine for it."

"A strike?" gasped Mommie. "How long is it going to last?"

"So we're staying?" asked Maggie.

"It shouldn't last too long," said Papa. "We'll stay long enough to get Dad to the doctor and then we'll head home to Michigan when he's a little better."

That Monday the diagnosis was a serious one. Grandpa

needed to have an operation. It was a hernia, a very fragile one. "I don't care what that doctor says." protested Grandpa. "I don't want to go to some hospital for them to cut me open and send me a big bill!"

For the time being, Grandpa got his way... and the strike endured.

****

It was the end of September. The mornings were becoming cool. One day, Grandma was feeling good and was quite agile with her crutches now that she no longer had a cast. She felt that Grandpa was well enough to leave alone for a day. "David, why don't we take a drive to the apple orchards." Grandma had peach trees, and a scrawny little crab apple tree, but not an orchard full of apples. The girls piled into the back of the station wagon as Mommie, Papa and Grandma got in. Maggie held tightly to the picnic basket. The trip seemed to take all day to the children, but in reality it was only late morning.

Before long, they were driving through rows and rows of orchards belonging to several farms. They stopped at a big whitewashed warehouse and got out of the car. Grandma leaned on her crutch and stood there looking over baskets and boxes of apples. There were red ones and blushing pink yellow ones. There were firm, green ones for pies, juicy and soft ones for cider and sauces. Grandma pointed to some yellow apples covered with faint freckles. "Yellow Delicious! Them's the best eatin' apples ever!" she said. She selected a bushel full of the yellow ones and a variety box of many colored apples. Papa, Mommie and the farmer put the apples in the back of the car and the family was on the road again.

This time they took a different route back. They drove through the Blue Ridge Parkway, over a winding and beautiful drive. Papa stopped the car at some picnic tables and Mommie carried the basket to one. Papa took out some red delicious apples since they were the closest to the back window. They sat and ate, enjoying the pretty day. The kids ran up and down the hills chasing each other and pretending to be Indians from many long years ago.

They looked at a log cabin, peering inside. They sat on the porch, playing with sticks, making miniature log cabins, until some other tourists walked up to take a look. Maggie and Lizzie ran in and out of the pastures and they climbed over split rail fences until they became tired. Then they went back to the cabin to look at some pretty moths clinging to the side of the wood logs.

When Papa said it was time to go, the children didn't hurry back to the car. Lizzie looked into the great blue sky with its bright, white puffy clouds, breathing in deeply. She was the last person to step into the station wagon.

They drove a little farther on the parkway and stopped at an old historic mill. It looked a lot like the picture in Grandma's sitting room. Lizzie even said so to Maggie. Grandma said, "Yes, that's the mill in my picture. It's older than I am!" Papa chuckled and posed the children for pictures. He tried to take pictures of Mommie and Grandma, but they just covered their faces with their hand bags and made jokes about breaking the camera. Papa managed to snap a picture of Mommie when she wasn't hiding. She was sniffing a pretty flower. Lizzie felt so happy. She began skipping around in the grass, then twirling. Maggie joined her and they danced around to music that was in their heads, the kind of song that only a child can hear in her heart. Suddenly Papa started hopping around, making funny faces at them. The girls squealed and giggled. He chased them back to the car and the family left.

Although the drive didn't seem as long on the way back from the mill, it was completely dark by the time they arrived home. After a late supper, Maggie helped Grandma make applesauce. They wiped the jars and put them in the pantry. Grandpa sat at the table with about a half dozen yellow delicious apples in front of him. He took out a paring knife from his pocket. Grandpa smiled quietly at Lizzie. His eyes looked moist and red. He blinked and nodded at the apples and took one in his hand. He slowly peeled it. The yellow skin came off in one long spiral. Lizzie played with the peel as Grandpa began to slice the fruit into small wedges. He handed one to Lizzie and took one for himself. This was the sweetest apple Lizzie had ever tasted! It even smelled delicious! They finished that apple and began another one, repeating the process of peeling and slicing. As they began the third apple, Maggie joined them at the table. The four of them finished the fruit together.

"Grandpa, don't you feel well?" asked Maggie.

"Well, my side just hurts bad," answered the old man.

"I think it's time you went to the hospital," said Grandma. "I'll call to make an appointment tomorrow."

Grandpa looked weary. "I won't say a word 'agin' it this time."

CHAPTER FOURTEEN

THANKFUL FOR WHAT WE'VE BEEN GIVEN

THERE SEEMED to be no end to the strike. Cumulative days turned into slow moving weeks. The weeks became dull months. Papa was itching to get back to work, but deep inside he was relieved that he wasn't at the factory just yet: Grandpa had the operation but still wasn't feeling better.

Less than two weeks before Thanksgiving, Lizzie hoped her plan to ask Papa if they could go to California would work. She had been saving up her pennies. It seemed like a lifetime to the little girl since she had seen her big sister Jenny. The weekend phone calls were no fun. Lizzie missed Jenny's hugs. She was so excited that with the little money she had saved they could have a big trip now, instead of waiting to see Jenny in the Summer.

Papa woke up from his nap and went to pick up Maggie from Sunday School. Lizzie asked to come along. She sat in the backseat, trying to count her pennies, but thoughts of playing with Jenny occupied her mind. Soon, Maggie came trotting out of the church. She got into the car. Lizzie decided to ask Papa about going to California but before the little girl could open her mouth, Maggie was telling him all about the story her teacher told the children. It was about an Indian named Squanto who had been to England and returned to find his entire tribe gone. They had all died while he was away. Maggie began to cry.

Lizzie asked, "Were they Cherokee?"

Maggie sobbed, "No."

"Then I don't care!" said Lizzie. Papa tried to stifle a chuckle.

Too soon they were back at Grandma's, so it wasn't until after lunch that Lizzie asked if they could go to California and see Jenny for Thanksgiving. Papa said, "I already told you, No."

Lizzie said, "Look at all the money I saved! We can go now."
Papa just smiled and said, "I think the union's getting ready
to sign a contract and I might be going back to work in a few
days. We'll be heading back to Michigan if all goes well."
Several days later, the strike was over, but Papa was not re-
turning to work. Grandpa had taken a turn for the worse. Lizzie's
dad was on the phone with his boss. "My father is very sick and
it doesn't look good," Papa said to the man on the other end. "I
might not be in to work until after Thanksgiving." He paused.
"No this isn't a ploy to get a few extra days of vacation for the
holiday. This couldn't have come at a worse time."

Uncle Edward and Auntie Lena arrived in Virginia that night.
Lizzie and Maggie went outside with Grandma when they heard
car doors slam. The air was crisp. There was a smell of chickens,
cows, hayfields and corn mingled with quartz clay. In the darkness, Auntie saw Kemo. His tail was wagging and he was nip-
ping at her feet. She noticed how large the dog was, larger than
any dog she had ever seen. "Mother, your dog is huge! He looks
like a wolf!"

Auntie Lena was Papa's big sister. She took Maggie's and
Lizzie's tiny hands as she went inside the house. Her kids were
all grown up but she remembered how to make little children
happy. Before it was time for the girls to go to sleep, Auntie
Lena read to Maggie and Lizzie and did puzzles with them. The
adults would use the beds, so Lizzie and Maggie were told that
night they would have to bed down under some blankets near
the wood stove. Auntie Lena comforted the girls, sang songs and
rocked them to sleep, setting them on the floor one at a time. She
covered them with soft blankets and tip-toed out of the room.

In less than a week, some time during the night, more relatives arrived: Uncle Gene, Aunt Merry and Aunt Della. Lizzie
found the adult conversation at breakfast tiresome. She excused
herself from the table and went into the bedroom. She found her
box of plastic cowboys and Indians in a closet. She and Maggie
played while more relatives entered the house. All the grownups
visited and asked about Grandpa.

They heard Grandma say, "Well, as you know, that pain turned out to be a hernia. The doctor said it had to be fixed. So, Roy had the surgery up in Richmond - at a good hospital. He was laid up there a long time. Then he came home and it got worse. He's all sick; all sick." She just shook her head.

"I just don't know why the old fool won't go back to the hospital!" said Jerry. "He's a stubborn cuss."

Papa said, "We should just carry him out to the car."

"Or call an ambulance," said Della.

"Won't do no good," insisted Grandma. "I told him he should go to the doctor and he says all they do is cut and prod and it hurts. He won't go."

"Then have a doctor come here," said Edward.

"The doctor said he'd come up for a house call first thing tomorrow morning. Today he fully intends to enjoy Thanksgiving Dinner with his family. He said if it was urgent, to take Roy to the hospital," answered Grandma.

"So we're back at square one," said Papa.

Merry came in from Grandpa's room. "He looks very pale and weak," she said.

"But, he says he wants us to have a normal Thanksgiving," Grandma stated.

"If that's possible, under these circumstances," said Della, raising her eyebrows.

The Thompson kids came over for a quick visit. They hadn't been to the farm since school started in September. Maggie and Lizzie followed the children out to the pond. "We can't play long," said Roberta.

Wendell said, "Look at them tadpoles! It's way too late in the season for them thangs' to be there!"

Darlene said, "Their mommas and papas were eaten up. Where'd they come from?"

Roger looked at the wriggling baby frogs and said, "Maybe there weren't any big 'uns to eat the eggs that were left and they just hatched. Besides, there were tadpoles in August."

"Those were the babies of the ones that got 'et' up," said Wendell.

"Yeah, but what laid *these* eggs?" questioned Darlene.

"I don't know!" yelled Roger.

As the older children watched the tadpoles gather in the mud, R.D. walked over to Lizzie and asked, "Are you having turkey?" Before Lizzie could answer, he said, "We slaughtered a hog. We're having ham. I can't wait!"

"I don't think they're a having anything," said Roger. "Their Grandpa's dying."

"Dying?" cried Lizzie.

"What?" screamed Maggie. Tears fell from her eyes and splashed into the pond from the dock.

Lizzie just shivered. "I didn't know," she sobbed.

R.D. took her hand and whispered, "You're 'pertier' now your hair is all growed out and curly again." He attempted to cheer up his little friend.

"Of course they're having Thanksgiving," said Roberta.

"I don't know what we're having," Lizzie said solemnly.

"Look at the time!" shouted Wendell looking at his watch. "We stayed too long!"

Roberta said, "It's time to go or we'll miss our dinner."

The children headed back to the farmhouse as clouds gathered and wind blew at them. The Thompsons walked the other way to go home. As the girls stepped inside everyone was gathering for supper. "We were just about to send someone out to look for you young 'uns," said Uncle Edward. "Didn't you hear us calling for you?"

"With that wind a blowin' I don't think they could hear," said Grandma.

Lizzie couldn't taste a thing. The turkey seemed dry and nothing else appealed to her. Auntie Lena asked, "What's wrong, my dear?"

Lizzie answered, "I'm not enthused with the turkey!"

"What a big word for a little girl," said Auntie Lena and everyone laughed. Lizzie didn't feel like laughing. She looked down at her plate.

"Is Grandpa dying?" asked Maggie.

"We don't know that," said Papa. "Let's not talk about it now," he said.

It seemed as if everyone was ignoring a large elephant in the room. Aunts, uncles and cousins talked about anything and everything. They didn't talk about Grandpa, lying in his bedroom. Sometimes Grandma or Aunt Merry would check in on him. He was breathing heavily one hour, sleeping like a quiet baby the next.

The men watched football on the little television and the ladies cleaned the dishes and put away all the food. "One things fer sure," said Grandma, "There won't be two weeks of leftovers with this crowd!"

"I don't know how you all could eat, with Roy dying in the next room!" cried Merry.

Everyone glared, motioning to the children. Grandma calmly said, "Roy wanted it that way. Besides, my Momma always said the living don't need to stop a'livin' for the dyin' of the dying."

"What do you mean?" asked Maggie.

Grandma turned to her granddaughter and said, "Life goes on. You have to keep a'livin' no matter what."

"Now, let's get these little ones to bed," said Auntie Lena. She scooped up a girl under each arm and tucked them into their makeshift beds. Lizzie felt that it was too early to go to sleep, but she was much too tired to protest.

CHAPTER FIFTEEN

COLD REALITY

FRIDAY MORNING was sunny despite the wind and cold from the day before. The farmhouse was quiet. Lizzie could hear the clanking of dishes and whispering from the kitchen, so she crawled out from under the blankets. Her toes became cold on the hard floor as she stepped quietly up to her father. "Why is everybody so quiet?" she asked.

"Grandpa didn't sleep too well last night." said Papa. "Now he's a little more comfortable so we are letting him sleep in." Within a short time, everybody was awake and it was hard to keep a house full of people completely quiet.

Doc Poston knocked on the front door and Della let him in. The doctor spent a while in Grandpa's room. Only Grandma went in with them. After the brief exam, he took Grandma alone into the living room and they sat and talked awhile. Their conversation was so soft that everyone strained to listen.

"Momma," said Jerry to Della, "I'm heading outside to feed the cattle." He rubbed his nose and grabbed his jacket.

Della walked over to Papa. "Maybe you could help him, Davey?" she said to her younger brother.

"He can handle it." said Papa.

"I'm not asking you, I'm telling you," said Della. "I know you boys don't get along. You were always the baby and then when I had Jerry, Mother doted all over him. I am telling you to help. Mother needs the chores done and you need to set aside this feud. Be a man, Davey."

Papa put on his jacket. "Della, I don't want any sore feelings, but Jerry is a sneaky, lowdown..."

"Enough," said Della. "Please, just set aside your feelings."

Before this, Lizzie didn't think Papa disliked anyone. The truth was he was so mad at Jerry that his own big sister had to boss him around like he was a little boy. Lizzie almost laughed out loud. Maggie asked her little sister to follow Papa outside with her. "We can get the eggs together. I saw the geese wandering by the pond when I looked out the window."

"Okay," said Lizzie. She knew deep down if there was any trouble, Papa would come and help. Most of all she wanted to see if Jerry and Papa would get into a fight. She imagined it would look a lot like a cowboy brawl; like in the movies she watched on Saturday afternoon TV.

As they were getting the eggs, they saw Doc Poston leave. They left the chicken yard, hastily placing the eggs in a basket, putting them high up on the propane tank. They ran off to follow Papa, their breath coming out in puffs of steam. Instead of catching up to their father, they ran into Auntie Lena and Mommie who were struggling to carry milk in four large pails. Tony stopped behind the women to lap up some of the milk that had sloshed over the sides. "C'mon, girls, help us carry this back to the house."

When they entered, several strange people were there. Auntie Della said they were all paying their last respects. Lizzie wasn't sure what that meant. Mommie helped the girls take their coats off. After that, the children were pretty much ignored. It was as if the people couldn't see the children. That made it easy for Lizzie to listen in on conversations. Then she heard Grandma's voice coming from the living room. Lizzie walked out of the kitchen, through the sitting room and down the tiny hall into the parlor. Grandma was telling some visitors, "Roy has some clots and if he's moved off the mountain he's a gonner. If this medicine works, there's a chance, but it doesn't look good."

"Now he's got the pneumonee' from staying in bed so long!" said Uncle Gene. "That would explain why he's been breathing so hard."

"At least he is home in his *own* bed and not in some cold hospital," moaned his wife, Aunt Merry.

Lizzie was very frightened. Her heart thumped in her little chest and felt like it was about to break. All day people came and went. Papa just said they should leave Grandpa alone to rest. Before long, the ladies were making turkey sandwiches and heating leftover yams and pies. The men moved tables into the sitting room.

In the commotion, nobody noticed Lizzie, her feet padding noiselessly into Grandpa's bedroom. The curtains were closed and the lights were off. The room was very dark. As Lizzie's eyes gradually adjusted to the blackness she listened to Grandpa gasping for air. His breaths had a gurgle in them. She tip-toed closer to the bed. She could see some things by now. She noticed Grandpa wasn't wearing his wire rimmed glasses. She saw, also, that he was drooling from the corners of his mouth. His eyes slowly opened and he gave her a weak smile, reaching out to hold his granddaughter. Lizzie quietly held her grandfather's hand, but no words were spoken. Grandpa fell back to sleep.

Lizzie quietly snuck back out of Grandpa's room and shut the door. Jerry found her hand on the doorknob. "Where do you think you're going?" he asked. "You're a bad little girl! You left the eggs outside! Kemo got every last one of them! You want him to turn into an egg-sucking dog? Huh? Then Grandma would have to shoot him!"

Papa pulled them both away from the door. "You want to wake Grandpa up?" he asked angrily. "I bet you knocked them eggs over out of spite, Jerry. Just leave my kid alone or I'll chop off your pinky finger and use it for fish bait!" Lizzie didn't know if Papa could really do something like that and she really didn't want to know. She just hoped Kemo wouldn't become an egg-sucking dog. She didn't want Grandma to shoot him.

After dinner, Grandma checked in on Grandpa and gave him some sips of water. "Still the same," she reported.

Merry walked into Grandpa's room close to bedtime. "He's breathing real hard."

Lizzie was put to bed on the floor but didn't sleep well. Maggie tossed and turned beside her. The lonely hours dragged on, as Lizzie saw the glow of light coming from the kitchen where most of the adults kept a death watch. She listened to the hushed voices and heard Uncle Edward say, "He's gone." The little girl heard crying and sighs.

Merry burst into tears, "I was the last to see him alive!"

Lizzie could hear bits of conversation as the clock ticked beside her. To the child's surprise, Mommie had been next to the girls all along. Lizzie felt her mother roll over as she said, "It's past four a.m.!" and stepped out from under the blankets to join the other adults.

Grandpa... dead. Lizzie didn't seem to understand. She wouldn't allow herself to. Grandpa was dead, like the bullfrogs, cows, Sassie, like...

Suddenly it was Saturday morning. Lizzie must have fallen asleep right after Grandpa passed away. The little girl looked out the window. The sun was fairly high up in the sky. She saw some men in a big, black car drive away. She didn't know who they were. She dressed and went outside. Kemo hung his head down low and sometimes looked up with big, sad eyes. He seemed to understand his master was not coming back.

Lizzie and Maggie had to gather the eggs again. The little girls wished the Thompson children would come by, but Papa said there was enough help with all the Aunts and Uncles around.

One grey, drizzly day blended into the next. People came and went all weekend. They would pick up pretty little Maggie and say what a beautiful child she was. Lizzie just hid in a corner and frowned.

Monday dawned as dreary as the weekend. Today was the day of the funeral. Lizzie had never seen Papa in a suit. It was a dark blue, navy color. Lizzie and Maggie wore dark blue, almost matching their father. At the funeral most of the mourners were in their Sunday best, but the colors were black, charcoal grey and other dark shades.

Papa and Mommie sat down with the girls and held them close. Lizzie looked around and tried to sit still. The room was the color of sky blue, with matching curtains and soft lights. Jillian and her family were there. She held tightly to Lizzie's hand and wouldn't let go until after the preacher ended his sermon. More people spoke and Lizzie stared into the back of another mourner. She studied the pattern of his suit.

****

The little girl found herself in the car as the family drove back to the farmhouse. Lizzie must have fallen asleep for a long time, because she didn't even witness the burial that everyone was talking about. More people came, some bearing dishes of comfort food. They would visit for a short time, and leave just as quickly. Cecil and his wife came in, carrying two dishes of banana pudding.

The phone rang. It was Jenny calling from California, crying. She was so miserable that she had to remain out west and miss the funeral. She sobbed on the other end for quite some time. Mommie reassured her the best she could.

After the call, Mommie walked her little girls to the bedroom. Lizzie felt like there was a huge lump in her throat, but she managed to ask, "Why did Grandpa die?"

"Because he was very sick, Lizzie," answered Mommie.

Maggie said, "Daddy had a hurt leg, Grandma had a broken leg, you got hurt bad and you all didn't die!"

Lizzie spoke up again, "I mean why did he *have* to die? Why does anyone have to die?" Tears quietly streamed down her cheeks. Mommie took the children into her arms and held them tight. They sat on the floor for awhile.

Mommie finally said, "Everything has to die sometime. Bodies get old and tired and finally give out. Some people give their lives before their time to save others. Soldiers and firemen risk their lives and sometimes die to rescue people."

"Jesus gave *his* life for us." said Maggie, in a matter-of-fact manner. "I learned that in Sunday School."

Mommie went on, "I guess if we lived forever here on earth, there wouldn't be enough room for the new ones being born."

Lizzie cried, "But what if I don't want any new babies?"

Mommie took Lizzie's face into her hands. The child could feel the tips of Mommie's long finger nails. Mother and child looked into each others' eyes. "You mean you wouldn't want to see anymore kittens, puppies or calves? You love puppies."

"...and I love little babies!" said Maggie. "I wouldn't want there to be no more babies in the world!"

"When something gets very old and tired, it's time for that body to take a long rest," explained Mommie. "The new people and horses and other creatures begin to take on the work of life. Like when a pair of blue jeans wears out, it's time for new ones. I know it's not exactly like that with people. You love people, like Grandpa, but it was time for his worn out body to rest. There won't ever be another Grandpa like Roy, but maybe someday your daddy can be a grandpa and I can be a grandma."

"When I have a baby someday or Jenny gets married and has a baby!" said Maggie with a big smile lighting up her face.

"Life goes on and everyone gets a turn at a new task," said Mommie.

Lizzie looked thoughtful. "It's like taking turns playing a game?" asked Lizzie.

"Yes, a very busy, complicated game that's known as living," Mommie said.

The girls remained silent after that. Mommie then got up off the floor to change Maggie and Lizzie out of their dresses. She hadn't washed any clothes for a few days. Somehow she managed to find something clean for Maggie. Mommie found some of Greg's clothes he had left behind in a drawer and dressed Lizzie in them. When Lizzie and Mommie walked out into the sitting room, Edward said, "Greg didn't get much wear out of those jeans. They're practically new. He left 'em here last summer."

Lizzie felt awkward. The jeans were loose. She sat down and listened to her aunts and uncles talking. "Hey, Davey, you got room for two more?" yelled Edward. "Della and Lena want to ride home with you because I have to head back in a couple hours. Gene and Merry are staying a few extra days to help out Mother."

Della spoke in a whisper. "I'm not really in a big hurry to get home. I just don't think I could stand to listen to another twelve plus hours of the same Elvis eight track over and over..."

"Della, you don't mean," gasped Aunt Lena.

"Yes, the whole way down," said Della. "I prayed to God that tape would break, and when it did, Merry bought another one at the next truck stop!" Lizzie had a big crush on Elvis and couldn't understand why her aunts complained.

From across the room and above the din of relatives' voices, Lizzie could hear Papa say, "Yes, we're leaving for Michigan about seven a.m. tomorrow. I have to get back to my job and start working this week. I promised my boss I'd be back as soon as I could. My job's on the line if I don't get back to the factory."

At that moment, Lizzie formed a plan from a place deep in the back of her mind. She always wanted to live on a farm. Papa promised her a horse. They planned to get chickens as soon as they settled into a house. Mommie said she was going to plant a garden and wanted a place that had apple trees in the yard. All their new home needed was some bullfrogs to sing them to sleep. So, the little girl grabbed an empty canning jar and headed out the door, dressed only in jeans and a t-shirt. It was a little chilly as she stepped onto the porch and patted Tony. Then the little girl crawled under the wooden gate, followed by Kemo. She skipped along the lower pasture and walked over the bridge, stopping momentarily to look in the stream. She climbed the high pasture, past the pond and looked back. The clouds were low over the hills and a thick mist gathered all around. She turned back to descend the hill and go back to the water.

Lizzie saw her breath coming out of her mouth, smoke-like in the air. She bent down over the bank and tried to catch some nearby tadpoles. She wasn't close enough to the water. Lizzie got closer to the edge and her toes felt wet. Time and again, she tried to reach out and scoop the little swimmers but all she got was a jar full of brown water and mud in her tennis shoes.

Frustrated, Lizzie walked around to the far side of the pond and watched some tadpoles gather together in the weeds near the edge of the water. She reached way over and scooped up five baby frogs. As she lifted the jar out, she slipped in the mud and landed in water up to her thighs. She crawled out of the muck and set her jar full of tadpoles down on the shore, leaving her jeans behind. She reached into the muddy water and grabbed her pants. Pulling them back on, Lizzie noticed that she had lost her right shoe in the pond. Carefully reaching in, she pulled out the dripping shoe and shook it off. Kemo began to whine beside her.

The child put her shoes back on her cold, wet feet. She felt an icy smack on her cheek followed by another! Cold, hard rain droplets were falling from the mist. It was beginning to sleet! Lizzie began to shiver. Her t-shirt was getting wet from the icy rain and her jeans were soaked through and clinging to her tiny legs. Kemo followed Lizzie as the little girl walked stiffly like a robot. She was beginning to freeze. Still her fingers clung to the jar. Before long, she neared the gate. Papa and Mommie were just about to open it when they saw their daughter.

"Everyone's been looking for you!" yelled Mommie.

Papa picked Lizzie up and carried her inside. "Don't pour out my pollywogs!" screamed Lizzie. Mommie set them on the porch.

"What happened?" gasped Grandma.

"I f-fell in the pond c-catching my new pets!" answered Lizzie. Maggie thought her sister sounded like Cecil.

"What you could have caught was your death!" cried Grandma.

Papa was too scared to scold his little girl. He and Maggie watched as Mommie filled the tub with warm water. Off came Lizzie's shirt and then the jeans. Lizzie's legs were blue and her teeth chattered. Papa asked, "Is that from the jeans? Did the dye stain her legs?" Once Lizzie had sucked on a red ribbon and got dye all over her mouth. Maybe this was the same thing, she thought.

Mommie said, "No, she's so freezing cold her legs are turning blue!"

They warmed her up in the tub and later rubbed her dry with the towels trying to get circulation back into her limbs. Then they took her to sit on Papa's lap by the wood stove. "We can't even take her to the hospital!" yelled Papa. "Look at that storm out there. Mother, you just can't live alone on top of this mountain! Not at your age!"

Then he looked down at the quiet child in his lap. "Don't you ever go to the pond alone again, Young Lady!"

"We could have lost you, too," said Grandma, tears welling up in her eyes.

Maggie just cried quietly and Mommie held her close. The aunts brought in some hot chocolate for the children. After a few sips, Lizzie said, "Can I keep the pollywogs?"

"Yes," Papa said, "...and don't you even dream of pouring them out, Jerry." Jerry drank his coffee and stood in the corner near his mother while everyone sat quietly listening to the fire crackling in the wood stove.

CHAPTER SIXTEEN

THE FIELD IS WHITE

THE FOLLOWING morning dawned cold and fresh. All around
the farmhouse was a thick blanket of snow. Lizzie had
never seen snow so clean! She looked out the window and
watched Kemo struggle in the drifts. He made great leaps from
the shed to the house. It was so deep, he couldn't walk easily
until he got to the porch. "Well I'll be!" said Grandma. "It's *never*
snowed like this here!"

Mommie said, "Doesn't it usually melt?"

"Yes, it does, by the time the sun comes through. This is highly
unusual," explained Grandma.

A snowplow came by at nine in the morning. It was a neighbor
that, as he said had, "...come by to dig Zonie out." Papa shoveled
the walk from the porch and all around the house to the drive.

Afterwards, Papa picked up the packaged beef that Grandma
had ordered. Sometime ago, a yearling calf from off the farm had
been butchered, processed and wrapped and was now waiting
in the butcher shop. Grandma said she couldn't use all that beef
by herself now. Between the funeral and Lizzie sliding into the
pond, the meat was nearly forgotten. They would have to keep
it in Uncle Edward's deepfreeze until they bought a freezer of
their own.

An hour later, Papa returned with the station wagon full of
meat. After taking enough out for Grandma, he glumly said,
"We're already running late. I don't think we're going to make
good time at all!"

As the family was about to get into the car, they saw Kemo
struggling to carry some large animal through the pasture. Jerry

97

and Uncle Gene were just coming back from doing the chores and saw it too. Kemo was carrying a dead calf.

"Well, look at that!" said Gene. "Looks like Kemo has a going away present for you!"

Papa said, "Sorry, Boy, we already got our meat at the butcher's this morning."

At that moment, a man drove up to the house in a pick-up. Grandma met him at the end of the drive thinking he was another person come to pay his respects. "So, that wolf is yours!" he said, not even introducing himself. "I've been following that beast from my farm and was about to shoot it when he got to your fence line!" The man was angry. "That animal stole that calf from off my farm!"

Grandma said, "Looks too small to be full term. It's a little early for calving. Kemo would never kill a calf. He's never hurt any of mine!"

Papa spoke up, "I bet your cow miscarried and Kemo just found the carcass in the field."

"Most likely," said the farmer, "but I don't like having such a dangerous dog around! Heck, I thought it was a wolf!"

Everyone looked at Kemo. He wagged his tail looking up proudly as he displayed the dead cow. Kemo really did look like a wolf. He was huge, with thick, grey fur, even between his large paws. "What breed is he?" asked the farmer.

"He's a German Shepherd," answered Papa.

"I used to breed Shepherds and train them in the service. That ain't no Shepherd," said the man looking at Papa and Grandma strangely. "I think you're hiding a wolf up here and I aim to tell the sheriff's department."

"Well, sir, we got this dog from the pound in Mount Airy and they didn't say anything about him being a wolf. He's a dog!" insisted Grandma. "You're new here, I think. The sheriff is good friends with my family. He's a reasonable man and he's never had any problems with our Kemo." Grandma paused and looked sadly at the sky as it was slowly clearing. "Besides, my husband just died and I'll be a moving off the mountain just as soon as I sell the place. You won't have any more troubles with my dog."

Grandma, turned around without even excusing herself and went in the house.

"Sorry to hear all about your troubles," said the farmer to the remaining family standing around, "but I don't *ever* want to see that wolf at my farm again!" He hastily threw the carcass into his truck bed. Kemo looked a little surprised but didn't snarl. The man got into his truck, rifle in hand, and drove off.

"I never thought about it before," said Papa. "Kemo is the largest German Shepherd that I ever did see and he was carrying a calf. I don't know any other dog that could do that."

Grandma came outside with a large paper sack full of sandwiches and put them in Mommie's arms. Everyone said a solemn, "Goodbye." Maggie carried Tony and got into the station wagon. Lizzie hugged Kemo, getting a little blood from his muzzle on the sleeve of her jacket. She lifted her frozen jar of tadpoles off of the porch and got in the car.

As the family drove through the path carved out by the snowplow, Lizzie and Maggie jumped up and over Aunties Lena and Della into the back of the station wagon atop the frozen beef that was covered by thick blankets. Maggie blew kisses and Lizzie waved her biggest goodbye ever, until they could no longer see Grandma nor Eureka Farm. The girls laid themselves out on the frozen meat until Maggie said, "My legs feel funny." Lizzie had a numb feeling like the one she felt the night before, walking from the pond.

Mommie said, "Oh, dear, the girls are going to freeze themselves to death!" She turned around and said, "Get up here!" She put quiet little Maggie between the aunts. Lizzie sat between her Mommie and Papa, Tony purring warmly on the little girl's lap.

They looked out over the misty hills with a silence so deep a soul could drown in it's depths. No one said anything until they crossed the state line. Deep in their hearts they all knew they would never see the farm again.

****

The following spring, Grandma sold her farm, bidding farewell to Cricket and the other cows. She moved off the mountain top, leaving the little community known as Meadows-of-Dan, Virginia, taking Kemo to North Carolina.

Many years passed by. The highway was widened and the little spring house was demolished, the quagmire covered over. Businesses moved in. The pond was drained. Time and progress grew where once peaches, corn and cattle thrived. Now there is a construction office and a flower shop where the farmhouse stood.

In the churchyard near Grandpa Roy's grave, the wildflowers grow at the edge of the woods. The deer peek shyly from behind the trees and life goes on.

Sometimes in Lizzie's dreams, she is walking up the great green hill, climbing over glittering quartz boulders followed by Sassie or Kemo as she breathes the fresh, clean air of Virginia. She dreams she is a little girl again.

About the Author

Virginia Elisabeth Farmer (Lizzie) grew up in Wayne County, Michigan. After highschool, she attended Brigham Young University in Provo, Utah majoring in Elementary Education. She has been writing since the mid 1980s. This is her first published book. Lizzie, or Liesa as her friends call her, still maintains a home in Michigan. She has a husband, two daughters and several cats.

Jared Beckstrand
ILLUSTRATION

At the age of 12 Jared began receiving commissions for his artwork. In 1990 he entered the field of animation as an asistant animator for Don Bluth Studios. A couple of years later he did work for Rich Animation Studios. He also created several coloring books for Western Publishing, a division of Golden Books. In 1994 he joined Walt Disney Feature Animation where he worked as a character animator for 10 years. In 2004 Jared embarked on a career in illustration and has done work for a variety of clientel. The majority of his time is now spent creating children's picture books, magazine illustration, editorial cartoons, caricatures, and logos.

Film credits

Walt Disney

Chicken Little
Tarzan
Hercules
Pocahontas
Emporer's New Groove
Fantasia 2000
Home on the Range
Treasure Planet
Hunchback of Notre Dame

Don Bluth

Thumbelina
Troll in Central Park
Pebble and the Penguin

Richard Rich

Swan Princess

Dimension Creative

Joanne Koltes
952-201-3981
jkoltes@visi.com

Artist
Jared Beckstrand
www.jaredbeckstrand.com